Emily Harvale lives in
– although she would prefer to live in the French Alps ... or Canada ... or anywhere that has several months of snow. Emily loves snow almost as much as she loves Christmas.

Having worked in the City (London) for several years, Emily returned to her home town of Hastings where she spends her days writing ... and wondering if it will ever snow.

You can contact her via her website, Facebook or Instagram.

There is also a Facebook group where fans can chat with Emily about her books, her writing day and life in general. Details can be found on Emily's website.

Author contacts:
www.emilyharvale.com
www.twitter.com/emilyharvale
www.facebook.com/emilyharvalewriter
www.instagram.com/emilyharvale

***

Scan the code above to see all Emily's books on Amazon

Also by this author

The Golf Widows' Club
Sailing Solo
Carole Singer's Christmas
Christmas Wishes
A Slippery Slope
The Perfect Christmas Plan
Be Mine
It Takes Two
Bells and Bows on Mistletoe Row

Lizzie Marshall series:
Highland Fling – book 1
Lizzie Marshall's Wedding – book 2

Goldebury Bay series:
Ninety Days of Summer – book 1
Ninety Steps to Summerhill – book 2
Ninety Days to Christmas – book 3

Hideaway Down series:
A Christmas Hideaway – book 1
Catch A Falling Star – book 2
Walking on Sunshine – book 3
Dancing in the Rain – book 4

Hall's Cross series
Deck the Halls – book 1
The Starlight Ball – book 2

Michaelmas Bay series
Christmas Secrets in Snowflake Cove – book 1
Blame it on the Moonlight – book 2

Lily Pond Lane series

The Cottage on Lily Pond Lane – four-part serial
Part One – New beginnings
Part Two – Summer secrets
Part Three – Autumn leaves
Part Four – Trick or treat
Christmas on Lily Pond Lane
Return to Lily Pond Lane
A Wedding on Lily Pond Lane
Secret Wishes and Summer Kisses on Lily Pond Lane

Wyntersleap series

Christmas at Wynter House – Book 1
New Beginnings at Wynter House – Book 2
A Wedding at Wynter House – Book 3
Love is in the Air – spin off

Merriment Bay series

Coming Home to Merriment Bay – Book 1
(four-part serial)
Part One – A Reunion
Part Two – Sparks Fly
Part Three – Christmas
Part Four – Starry Skies
Chasing Moonbeams in Merriment Bay – Book 2
Wedding Bells in Merriment Bay – Book 3

Seahorse Harbour series

Summer at my Sister's – book 1
Christmas at Aunt Elsie's – book 2
Just for Christmas – book 3
Tasty Treats at Seahorse Bites Café – book 4
Dreams and Schemes at The Seahorse Inn – book 5
Weddings and Reunions in Seahorse Harbour – book 6

Clementine Cove series

Christmas at Clementine Cove – book 1
Broken Hearts and Fresh Starts at Cove Café – book 2
Friendships Blossom in Clementine Cove – book 3

Norman Landing series
Saving Christmas – book 1
A not so secret Winter Wedding – book 2
Sunsets and surprises at Seascape Café-book 3
A Date at the end of The Pier – book 4

Locke Isle series
A Summer Escape – book 1
Christmas on Locke Isle – book 2

Betancourt Bay series
That Mistletoe Moment – book 1
That Winter Night – book 2
That Special Something – book 3
That Summer Hideaway – book 4
That Secret Wish – book 5

ISBN 978-1-917227-02-5

Published by Crescent Gate Publishing

Print edition published worldwide 2024
E-edition published worldwide 2024

Cover design by JR and Emily Harvale

Acknowledgements

My grateful thanks go to the following:

My webmaster, David Cleworth who does so much more than website stuff.
My cover design team, JR.
Luke Brabants. Luke is a talented artist and can be found at: www.lukebrabants.com
My wonderful friends for their friendship and love. You know I love you all.
All the fabulous members of my Readers' Club. You help and support me in so many ways and I am truly grateful for your ongoing friendship. I wouldn't be where I am today without you.
My Twitter and Facebook friends, and fans of my Facebook author page. It's great to chat with you. You help to keep me (relatively) sane!

To all my wonderful readers.
I hope your own secret wishes
come true. Xxx

Emily Harvale

That Secret Wish

From motorway
18
19
London Road
Wood Lane
17
13 14 15 16
Oak Street
Oak Street
London Road
8
12
Oak Street
7
9
10
11
Folkestone Road
Farm Lane
Grifforde Way
Folkestone
Betancourt Street
6
4 5
2 3
Betancourt Street
1
Locke Isle
Betancourt Bay

MAP KEY – BETANCOURT BAY

1) **Lookout Point** – At **310 feet**, this is the highest point on the white cliffs around Betancourt Bay. You can see Locke Isle from here while seated on the bench, and on a very clear day, even the coast of France. **Lookout Steps** lead down to the sandy beach – but there are **300 steps**, so most people access the beach farther along, where the cliff paths aren't so steep and there are fewer steps.
2) **Sunnycliff Cottage - James and Margaret Hart** live here. They have two daughters, **Fiona and Naomi.** Fiona lives in Folkestone with her husband, Greg Carter. Naomi is single and lived in Lewisham, but moved back to Betancourt Bay in Book 3 and has moved into the flat above Betancourt Bay Café with her boyfriend, Lucas Dove. She now owns both the flat and café, having purchased it from The Betancourts with her Lottery winnings.

3) **Willow Cottage** – Home to **Malorie Blackwell**, a reflexologist.
4) **Seaview Cottage** – **Laurence Lake** lives here. He's a successful author of several cosy crime books.
5) **Rosehip Cottage** – **Jean and Victor Mills** live here. Their four children, **Tom, Rob, Zoe and Tara** have all moved away but they come home for high days and holidays.
6) **Betancourt** – Ancestral home to the Betancourt family. **Archie Betancourt** has two sons, **Grifforde (known as Griff)** and **Russell**. Archie's second wife, Bianca (his first wife Francesca, died) has now gone to live with friends, and Archie plans to divorce her. Griff has taken over the running of the house and small estate, and Grace Eversley has moved in with him. He proposed and they are now planning their wedding. Russell spends a lot more time in London, but often returns to Betancourt.

7) **Mr and Mrs Bernard and Barbra Brimble's B & B** – **Barbra** describes herself as 'a people person'; people describe her as 'a nosy gossip' – but not to her face. She loves to sing, and often does, whether others want her to or not.
8) **Clifftop Farm** – Once part of the Betancourt's estate, but now a small holding owned by **Sandy and Sonia Grey**, most of the farmland having been sold-off by various Betancourts over the years. Sandy and Sonia are known for taking in all sorts of waifs and strays, both human and animal.
9) **The Royal Oak** pub – Although highly unlikely, legend has it that King Richard (The Lionheart) once sat beneath the ancient oak tree opposite the pub, on his way to join the Crusades. Owned and run by **Freddie Tollard** and his daughter, **Charlotte (Charlie)**

10) **The White House** – Home to **Simon and Patience (Pat) Eversley** and daughters **Grace** and **Hope** along with their dog, **Lady Elizabeth, known as Lady E**. The Eversleys run an Events company, **Eversley Events** from here.
11) The Rectory – **The Reverend Brian Copeland** and his wife **Daisy** live here.
12) **St Gabriel's Church** – with a bijou village hall attached. The church was built in 1086, the hall in 1946.
13) **Catkin Cottage** – Home to **Hanna Shaw**, an artist.
14) **Acorn Cottage** – Elderly sisters, **Rita and Vera Boot** have lived here all their lives.
15) **Bluebell Cottage** – **Greg Bishop** lives here. He owns a bookshop in Folkestone.
16) **Oak View Cottage** – **Molly Law** has recently inherited this cottage from her grandmother, **Millicent**. Molly lives in Folkestone with her parents, **Owen and Nikki**.

17) **Betancourt Bay Café** – Formerly leased to **Derek Dunpole** and his (miserable) wife, **Doris**, who had much grander plans than running a café in a small village, as she constantly reminded her long-suffering husband. They've now moved to Spain and Naomi Hart has bought it from the Betancourts who owned the freehold.
18) **West Wood** – owned by the Betancourts but they allow the villagers to use it.
19) **East Wood** – also owned by the Betancourts, who allow the villagers access.

Wish you were here?

This new series is set in Betancourt Bay, a fictional, clifftop village a mile from Folkestone. I've, sort of, 'demolished' everything that currently occupies this space in real life, and 'built' Betancourt Bay there instead. Apologies for that, but it was a necessary evil in order for me to tell these stories.

In addition to this, I have added a few fictional things/places/businesses in Folkestone – like the slipway where the Locke Isle Ferry docks, among others, so please forgive me for that!

This series also links to my other new series, Locke Isle, which is set on the fictional island of Locke Isle, two miles off the Kent coast, and also partly in the real town of Folkestone.

So if you know Folkestone and the surrounding area, you may not entirely recognise it when you read these books...

With love,
Emily xx

One

'Why, if it isn't Hanna Shaw! We haven't chatted for ages. Oooh. That's a pretty painting, dear.'

Hanna jumped at the sound of Barbra Brimble's voice. Not because of who had spoken (although Mrs Brimble was a notorious gossip and was best avoided if possible – and Hanna had successfully done so for months) but because she'd been so deep in thought that she hadn't seen the woman coming, and the shock of finding Barbra standing so close, startled her.

It had been the perfect summer morning – until then – and Hanna was enjoying both the glorious sunny weather, and the solitude.

When she'd left Catkin Cottage, the early morning air was cool, and on arrival, minutes later, at the ornate iron gates of Betancourt, the ancestral home of the Betancourt family, tiny droplets of dew clung to the tips of the recently mown grass on which she'd set up her easel. Autumn might be weeks away, and summer only halfway through, yet Hanna had needed a cardigan first thing in the morning.

Three hours later, with the sun a golden ball high in a clear cerulean sky, and the cardigan long since discarded, Hanna basked in the mid-morning heat and her hair danced around her shoulders in the gentle, summer breeze. Birds tweeted and chirped from the trees and bushes behind the stone walls of Betancourt, a butterfly or two flew by, and somewhere in the distance, a dog barked, while Hanna painted and daydreamed outside the gates of the stately home she loved.

Now Hanna instinctively took a step away from Barbra as her breathing returned to normal.

'Thank you,' she said. And then she spotted that the butterfly she had been adding to her painting of Betancourt and its grounds, as a finishing touch, now had a rather long tail.

Damn Barbra Brimble. Hanna would need to paint that out.

'I was thrilled to bits for young Grace Eversley,' Barbra said, leaning closer to Hanna in a conspiratorial fashion, 'when I heard the news of the engagement. And now there's going to be a wedding so soon after.

Between you and me, a few people thought the rush meant there might be a little Betancourt on the way. Well, you know how some people gossip, dear, and Grace did move into the house very quickly. But that's not so, apparently.'

'No it's not.' Hanna tried to retain her composure but her tone was sharp, even to her ears. Hanna had heard that rumour, and she had a fairly good idea who had started it. The woman standing right beside her. 'It's simply because they're so deeply in love and they can't wait to be husband and wife.'

Barbra was giving her an odd look. 'You don't sound too happy about that, dear.' Ignoring Hanna's tut of irritation, she continued. 'But then Grifforde Betancourt broke so many hearts when he announced on Christmas Eve that he loved Grace.'

'I'm truly happy for them,' Hanna snapped, wishing the woman would just go away and let her finish her painting of the gorgeous stately home and grounds.

'Of course, dear. If you say so. I'll admit I was astonished when I heard that Grifforde had apparently been in love with Grace for years. Weren't you? I hadn't guessed for one second that the gorgeous man felt that way about her. They had always seemed to dislike one another. And she was in love with poor dear Russell, or so she always said. Yes. It was a complete surprise. And I'm not the only one who thought so. But then who wants the younger brother if you can get the older one. Especially as it's Grifforde who inherits Betancourt.'

'What do you mean by that? It's not about the money. Or Betancourt. Grace adores Griff. And Russell is just as great as his older brother. We don't choose who we fall in love with.'

Hanna was growing angry, but she wouldn't let Barbra Brimble spoil her day. Instead, she focused her attention on the house and how beautiful it looked with the sunshine bringing out the warmth of the sand-coloured stonework, and how the tips of the trees swayed to and fro in the gentle breeze. The scents of so many varieties of flowers in the rows of flowerbeds lining both sides of the wall surrounding the grounds, mingled together, and wafted towards her, and she breathed in the heady fragrance, calmer now as Barbra's voice droned on and on in the background.

'Of course we don't dear. But for Grace to get Grifforde to propose so soon after they'd started dating was a triumph, wasn't it? And now the wedding! And all within eight months. Grifforde's a real catch, isn't he? Grace wouldn't want to let him slip away. So handsome. So rich. So rugged. Not to mention ... so sexy.' She giggled. 'Imagine being his wife. Why, it's like a fairytale, isn't it? Betancourt has stood here for centuries. Imagine the stories it could tell. Imagine all the things that have gone on within those walls. Imagine living in that magnificent house.' Barbra let out an envious sigh.

Distracted, Hanna matched it. She had been thinking something along similar lines before Barbra had appeared and interrupted her daydreaming. 'I do imagine it,' she said, absentmindedly. 'It would be a dream come true.'

It was a moment or two before she realised that Barbra had stopped talking, and the look the woman was giving her now was even more curious. Not to mention, slightly worrying. The raised brows, the sparkle in those all-seeing eyes, and the huge, almost triumphant smile that crept across Barbra's florid face sent an odd sort of shiver down Hanna's spine.

When Barbra laid a cold hand on Hanna's arm, she felt as though the woman was a spider who had just caught Hanna in her web.

'Oh, absolutely, dear,' said Barbra, with excitement in her voice. 'Now I must get on. I've interrupted you and your painting. You're such a talented artist ... although ... should that butterfly have that long, thick tail? It looks a bit like a dragon. But I'm sure you know best. I'll leave you be. Bye, bye.'

'Erm … No, I was…' The woman was gone before Hanna had finished her sentence.

Clenching her teeth and scowling at Barbra as the woman hurried away, she added. 'The only dragon around here, is you, Barbra Brimble.'

But that wasn't really fair to dragons, and despite being fully aware that dragons were fictional creatures, Hanna silently apologised to them as she set about removing the long tail from the butterfly in her painting.

Two

Russell Betancourt knew a thing or two about unrequited love, and how humiliating it was to have everyone in Betancourt Bay talking about you. He'd been hopelessly in love with Hope Eversley for years and had been foolish enough to declare his feelings for her on Christmas Eve, the same night that his older brother, Griff, had announced his own love for Hope's older sister, Grace. Unfortunately for Russell, whilst Grace gleefully admitted that she loved Griff, and they had spent the night in each other's arms at The Mistletoe Dance, Hope did not return Russell's feelings for her. He had spent the night drowning his sorrows while putting on a brave face, and mingling with the throng of guests enjoying themselves in his home.

Hope had been kind, and she had let him down as gently as she could, and somehow, they had remained friends, as they had been for all their lives. But it had been painful for

Russell to be friends with someone he loved, who didn't feel the same about him. He needed to get over Hope and had decided to spend less time at Betancourt and more time in the apartment the family owned in London.

And then in February, Hope had fallen in love with someone else.

Russell had only returned to Betancourt for Griff's proposal to Grace, at Griff''s request, which was also in February, and at Easter for the Grand Opening of Betancourt Bay Café. Everyone in the village had attended that.

People couldn't help who they fell in love with, Russell knew that, but even he was astonished when he heard the latest village gossip, within minutes of returning home to Betancourt for the first time since Easter.

He had just walked into the Great Hall, shortly after noon and, he had hoped, just in time for lunch, when Tabby, the housekeeper, had come to welcome him home.

'I'm so pleased to see you, Russell. We've all missed you,' she said, hurrying towards him.

He beamed at her. 'Hello, Tabby. Still here? I'm delighted you've decided to stay on, and not retire again. Betancourt wouldn't be the same without you.'

She had smiled at that as she always did when he teased her about her retirement. After a lifetime of working for the Betancourts, she had retired the previous year, but fortunately for the family, she had been persuaded to return within weeks, and had been back at Betancourt ever since. Even if she did now only work part-time.

Tabby had clucked at him like a hen. 'Betancourt will always be Betancourt whether I'm here or not. But it's not the same when you're away.'

Russell had taken her arm and linked it through his. She was more like a grandmother than an employee, and all the Betancourts loved her, and treated her as family.

'I've missed you too, Tabby. And this place.'

He glanced up at the stunningly beautiful chandelier hanging in the Great Hall as he and Tabby wandered towards the large, central staircase. He tossed his holdall to one side of the staircase and continued with Tabby to the kitchen.

'Will you be staying for the rest of the summer, or is this just a flying visit, like your last trip home at Easter?'

He had intended to return for a short visit in June, but work had kept him surprisingly busy, meaning he had changed his plans.

The Betancourt's thriving auction house in London, the offices of which were in a rather grand former home in the heart of Mayfair, usually ran like clockwork whether he or his brother were there or not. Their father had effectively left the running of the business to both Griff and Russell now that he had retired, and the running of the ancestral home, to Griff, as he was the next in line. But the family had been selling fine arts and antiques, books, wine, and jewellery for around two hundred years, and the Betancourts were really figureheads these days.

Throwing himself back into the business over the last few months though had helped Russell get over Hope, and a new client specifically asking for Russell's expertise in June, had reminded him how much he enjoyed the work.

Plus, travelling all over the world on business, never got old as far as Russell was concerned.

But nothing would keep him away from Betancourt during the first week of August.

'I'll be here for a week. Maybe two. I'm home for the Summer Fayre, of course, but I may stay a little longer. And I'll be back for the wedding, obviously, and standing in for Griff while he and Grace are on their honeymoon. We all know Dad is no longer interested in running the house. Although I may get roped in to help out between now and the wedding, so perhaps I'll stay for the remainder of the summer. I can pop back up to London if I'm needed.'

He doubted he would be now that the new client was happily on board and had signed a contract with Betancourt's auction house for the sale of his collection of exceedingly valuable paintings to go under the hammer in a forthcoming sale.

'I do hope you'll stay,' Tabby said.

Russell had known Tabby all his life and he could tell there was something on her mind.

'Why are you looking so anxious, Tabby? Is something wrong?'

'Oh, I'm sure it's nothing,' Tabby said, her expression saying the opposite as Russell opened the kitchen door and waited while she entered. 'You know how gossip spreads in this village.'

'Better than most,' he replied, remembering only too well what the gossips had said about him during those difficult months since Christmas. And the tongues had wagged again at Easter when he had chatted with Hope and her new boyfriend, Tom. Although as he'd been spending the majority of his time in London for the past few months, he'd missed a great deal of the gossip about him, and had assumed it had now died down.

Tabby had given him a sympathetic smile. 'Of course,' she said. 'And you know that, like everyone in this house, I take it all with a pinch of salt and dismiss it for what it is. One or two people with nothing better to do than talk about other people, whether what they say is true or false. But ... well ... this is a bit of a worry. Especially as Hanna is a good friend of both Griff and Grace.'

'Hanna? Hanna Shaw? What on earth can people be saying about Hanna? Everyone likes her.'

Tabby had thrown him a look. 'Everyone likes you, yet that didn't stop them all chattering, did it? And we all like Hope. But all the tongues wagged about her too. And they still are, now that she ... Oh. I didn't mean to mention Hope. I'm sorry, Russell.'

He had given her a reassuring smile. 'Don't worry, Tabby. My heart is almost entirely back together now. It's just missing one teeny tiny bit. And that will slot back in place when I fall in love with someone else. Which I shall. I'm finally sure of that. So you can mention Hope Eversley as often as you like, without me turning into a blubbering wreck. They say absence makes the heart grow fonder but in my case, absence was the best cure.'

'I'm so pleased you're doing so well. But you've never been a blubbering wreck and you never could be. You're far too strong for that. Griff may take after your dear, departed mother in looks, while you take after Archie, but you've both got her strength of character, and her kind and caring heart. Shall I make some tea?'

'I'd rather have a cold beer.' He hurried to the fridge before Tabby could get there. 'Which I'm more than capable of getting for myself.' He winked at her as he removed the top and tossed it into the recycling bin. Then he strolled over to the solid, ancient oak table and pulled out a chair. 'As luck would have it, I saw Hope and Tom walking hand-in-hand up Oak Street just now as I arrived, and we all waved at one another. I can safely say I didn't feel a pang of jealousy. And I must admit, they do look happy together. The perfect couple.'

'Yes,' said Tabby, making herself a cup of tea while he spoke, and then joining him at the table. 'They do seem perfect for one another. I hear they might be buying Oak View Cottage. Or at least, Tom might be buying it, and Hope might be moving in with him. And that's not gossip. Pat Eversley told me that in person, so if Hope's mum says that's what's happening, then it probably is.'

'Oak view Cottage?' Russell furrowed his brows. 'Wasn't that the one the Law family owned? Millicent Law lived there, didn't she? Oh, but she died this year. I suppose her son owns it now. He and his wife and daughter live in Folkestone, if I remember correctly.'

'That's right. But Millicent left the cottage to her granddaughter, Molly. And Molly has been renting it out. A lovely young woman called Jemma is living there at the moment. She's a famous author, like Laurence Lake. Only she writes historical romance novels, not cosy crime. Her books have been made into a hugely popular TV series. But I don't suppose you've watched it.' Tabby grinned at him knowingly.

Russell grinned back. 'No. But I'll add it to my list.' She knew him well enough to know that he didn't watch much TV, and when he did, it certainly wouldn't be a TV series based on historical romance novels.

'Oh, and she's dating Greg Bishop,' Tabby added. 'The lovely young man who lives next door to Oak View Cottage and who owns Bishop's Books in Folkestone.'

'Yes. I know Greg, Tabby. Although I didn't know he was dating someone. Griff didn't mention it.'

'Jemma only arrived in June. She was supposed to be here for one month but she decided to stay on for longer. She and Greg have only recently made it public knowledge that they're a couple. Of course there were rumours so everyone knew before they announced it.' Tabby rolled her eyes. 'And you only have to look at them to see they're madly in love. Anyway, Molly had gone on a cruise with her parents, and when she returned, she said it was her intention to sell Oak View Cottage. She's planning to work on a cruise ship and travel the world, so I hear.'

'Good for her. She won't have any trouble selling the cottage if Tom doesn't buy it. Property in this village is always in demand. In fact, Tom might find himself in a bidding war.'

Tabby nodded sagely. 'Yes. Some people thought Jemma would buy it, and she did say she was interested, but then we discovered that Greg made Jemma an offer of his own, just this last weekend. But not quite the same sort of offer.' Tabby grinned over the rim of her teacup. 'He's asked her to marry him. After only knowing her for a little less than two months. Can you believe that? It was love at first sight for both of them, it seems. They've gone away for a week to celebrate. But when they return, Jemma will be moving in with Greg. Which means that Tom won't have to compete with Jemma for the cottage. And, as I said, Pat Eversley told me yesterday that the offer Tom made Molly has been accepted. So, assuming the sale goes ahead, Tom and Hope will move into Oak View Cottage before too long.'

'Well it's all been happening while I've been away, hasn't it?'

'You have no idea.' Tabby rolled her eyes and grinned again. 'Gossip has been flying left, right, and centre. One day it's one thing and the next it's another.' The grin quickly faded.

'Ah yes. And speaking of gossip. You were saying the latest gossip is about Hanna, weren't you? And that it was a bit of a worry because she's friends with Grace and Griff. Although why would it matter about that? They couldn't care less about what the gossips might say.'

'Ordinarily, that would be true.' Tabby now twisted her teacup between her fingers in an oddly nervous fashion. 'But this latest piece of gossip is somewhat different. I heard it from Daisy Copeland when I called her this morning to check when the Reverend was free next week to have a final chat with Grace and Griff about their wedding rehearsal. And we all know that, as the vicar's wife, Daisy detests falsehoods. Although she is rather partial to a juicy bit of gossip. She heard it from Barbra Brimble herself, who had only left Hanna's side, minutes before. Barbra was attending one of Daisy's regular

Wednesday coffee mornings, and I phoned just as it was coming to an end, about two hours ago.'

'So what you're saying is the gossip is fresh and as it's only been passed between two people, it hasn't been embellished.'

'Exactly. Hanna just came right out and said it. Although Barbra did tell Daisy, who told me, that Hanna might not have realised she had spoken the words aloud. She was on the grass embankment outside the front gates this morning, painting a picture of Betancourt and the grounds when Barbra stopped for a chat. Barbra said she hadn't seen Hanna for months, and had been wondering if there was something wrong, and now she knows there is. Anyway, she said they discussed Grace and Griff and the upcoming wedding, and how wonderful it would be to live in Betancourt and to be Griff's wife, and that's when Hanna said it. She told Barbra that she thought of little else. That she longed to be married to Griff and often imagined that she was. That it would be a dream come true.'

Now Russell wished he hadn't asked and it took him a minute or two to fully comprehend what Tabby was telling him. That Barbra Brimble had heard it with her own ears that very morning and from Hanna's own lips. And Hanna was right outside the front gates of Betancourt, painting a picture of the house and grounds at the time. The house Hanna had said she wanted to live in and that it would be a dream come true.

And that she wanted to live in it with Grifforde Betancourt.

As Griff's wife.

Could this be true?

Was Hanna Shaw in love with his older brother, Griff?

Three

Grace Eversley didn't take much notice of the village gossip, and never had, although, like all the other residents, she had to admit that she quite liked hearing what the latest bit of gossip was and who it was about. But this time she wasn't thrilled to hear it. Neither was her fiancé, Griff, although, unlike Grace, he stated that he didn't believe it.

'It can't be true, can it?' Grace asked, when she had relayed to Griff what her sister, Hope, had told her less than an hour before. 'Hope only told me because she knows too well what a few words from Barbra Brimble can do. The woman almost split Hope and Tom up with her gossip. Although ... what Barbra told Tom was sort of true. At least in part. And that's the problem. What if even part of this is true?'

Griff leant back in his chair, a thoughtful expression on his face, replacing the initial surprise she had seen there. He had been working in his study when Grace had burst in, plonked herself in a chair on the other side of his desk, and said she needed to speak with him, urgently and in private. He had made a joke about it at first but once he'd quickly seen that she was serious, he'd listened to her intently.

'It's not true, Grace, I'm certain of that,' Griff said, sitting upright now. 'We're good friends, that's all. Yes, we joke and tease each other, but Hanna has never done anything to make me think for one minute that what she feels for me is more than friendship. I think we should simply ignore it.'

'That's easy for you to say. But let's not forget, Griff, you were in love with me for years, and I had no idea until you told me. Well, until you kissed me. You didn't tell me you'd been in love with me for most of your life, until Christmas Eve. But don't you see? You were able to hide your true feelings from me. What if Hanna is able to hide her true feelings from you? From both of us. Because I had no idea how she felt about you either.'

Griff frowned at that. 'I suppose that's true. I did hide my feelings from you. But don't forget, that's why I spent most of my time in London and only came home briefly and on rare occasions. I knew I wouldn't be able to keep my feelings to myself if I saw you on a regular basis. We see Hanna almost every day. Do you honestly believe that neither of us would've seen a slight hint of how she is supposed to feel? A look? A gesture? A word?'

Grace shrugged. 'I don't know. The thing is, I only have eyes for you, so I don't really take much notice of anyone else. I probably shouldn't admit that because it sounds as if I ignore everyone but you, and I don't. Not exactly.'

Griff smiled, got to his feet, and went to Grace, pulling her upright, and into his arms.

'And I only have eyes for you, my darling, so I know precisely what you mean. Yet I still think one of us would've spotted something. Wouldn't we?'

Their eyes met and they laughed even though it wasn't funny.

'No, Griff. I only see you.'

'And I only see you, Grace. You're right. However, I don't believe Hanna is in love with me. And even if she were, I'll only ever love you. You do know that, don't you?' He held her a little away from him and looked her directly in the eyes.

'I do. But what if she does love you? We've seen how painful it's been for Russell. Seeing us together and so much in love must be painful for Hanna.'

His arms dropped to his sides. 'If she loved me, yes. But she doesn't. I'm certain of that.'

Grace let out a sigh, turned and took a few steps away and then turned back and paced in frustration.

'Then why did she tell Barbra Brimble, of all people, that she does? She knows what the woman is like. So if she told Barbra, that must mean it's true. It also means she doesn't care if people know it. And what does that mean? That she wants you to know it's true? If that's the case, it makes things very awkward, Griff. How can we have her here as often as we do if all the time, she's yearning for you? If she's jealous of me and wants to be with you, that's going to make things uncomfortable between us, isn't it? Now that we know. And she will know that we know. Because one thing everybody knows is true, is that if you want everyone in Betancourt Bay to know something, you tell Barbra Brimble.'

He perched on the edge of his desk and let out a sigh of his own.

'Yes. But it's also true that Barbra tends to ... make things up. Not everything she says is true, Grace.'

'I know. But it's also true that Barbra hears things that others don't.'

Griff shook his head. 'And it's equally true that what Barbra thinks she's heard isn't always exactly what was said. She does have a tendency to embellish things rather a lot.'

Grace tutted. 'Yes. I know she's a dreadful gossip who doesn't let the truth stop her from telling a good tale. I don't know why anyone listens to her.' She threw him a sheepish smile and dropped onto the arm of the chair in which she was previously seated. 'But I'm as bad as everyone else. I was thrilled when I heard about Jemma and Greg. And also when I heard that Molly Law was selling Oak View Cottage. Although Hope was even more thrilled about that, as was Tom.' She stood up and walked towards the window. She couldn't quite see Oak View Cottage from here but it was close enough. 'I'm so glad they'll be buying it and moving in very soon. With Tom renting that house in Folkestone, I see so much less of Hope than I'd like. With her back in the village, we'll all get to spend more time together again.' She smiled as she turned back to face Griff. 'Mum and Dad are over the moon.'

'I can imagine,' Griff said. 'And I'm happy too. Mainly because it makes you even happier.'

She beamed at him but then frowned as a thought struck her. 'But that reminds me. Hope told me about something Jemma had said to her a couple of weeks ago. Do you remember that night that you and I first met Jemma? The night Hanna asked if she could bring Jemma here because she had been telling Hanna how much she wanted to see Betancourt.'

'I do remember our first meeting with Jemma was here, but other than that, I don't recall anything specific about that night. Oh, except how much Jemma adored the house. We said she could spend the night here and I've never seen anyone so happy to be told they could stay here for a night. I do remember that.'

'Yes. Well, Jemma told Hope that Hanna had told her she'd be thrilled when she saw you. And that later, she and Hanna were discussing how you were like a hero from one of Jemma's books, and that with your dark hair and intense dark eyes, you were the sort of man every woman dreams of being ravished by, and that every woman would long to tame you. Hanna told Jemma, who then told Hope, that she could see why so many women had fallen for you over the years, and Jemma said that, if she hadn't already fallen for Greg, she would've added herself to that list. So you see! Hanna had already told Jemma that she was in love with you.'

Griff frowned as if he hadn't fully understood what Grace was saying, but then he smiled and shook his head.

'As delighted as I am to receive such

lavish praise, if anything, all that tells us is that Jemma thinks I resemble one of her fictional heroes, and that Hanna agrees. Hanna told us she's a fan of Jemma's books. The words 'in love' weren't mentioned in any of that.'

'Sometimes the actual words aren't necessary. Everything else you say or do, says it all.'

Griff grinned mischievously as he took a few steps towards her.

'Really? So you're saying I don't need to tell you I love you, every single day? I can merely show you I do.'

'Yes. No. I mean ... of course you don't have to tell me every day, and you know you don't.' She sashayed up to him. 'But I do love it when you do.'

He wrapped her in his arms. 'Then I'll continue to do so. I love you, Grace Eversley. And only you. With all my heart.'

'And I love you, Griff Betancourt.'

The kiss they shared lasted for several minutes, and might have led to a lot more than kissing if another thought hadn't struck Grace. She pulled away from him.

'I've remembered something else that Hope told me.'

Griff sighed. 'I'm beginning to think that Hope talks too much. Sorry, darling. I can see you're not amused by that. What else did

Hope tell you?'

'It's about that gorgeous painting Hanna did. The one of us dancing in the Great Hall on Christmas Eve at The Mistletoe Dance. The painting Hope and my family, and yours … and Hanna, gave us at our engagement party.'

'I know the painting, Grace. It's currently hanging in our bedroom. I'm unsure of the point you're trying to make. It clearly shows anyone who may look at it, how deeply in love we were with one another that night. And as Hanna painted it, I think that proves my point. Plus, anyone who knows us as well as Hanna does, knows our love has only grown deeper and stronger since then, so I'm not sure why Hope mentioning that painting is bothering you right now.'

'It's bothering me because Hope told me that she didn't ask Hanna to paint it. It was already done, and sitting in Hanna's studio in Catkin Cottage. Hope saw it when she went upstairs to use the loo that night she was drinking wine at Hanna's. She asked Hanna about it and whether it was for sale and Hanna said it just needed a few finishing touches, or something like that. Anyway, my point is, what if the woman in the painting wasn't me?'

Griff frowned. 'But it is you, darling. Anyone can see that.'

'It is me now. Yes. And obviously when we received it, it was me. But what if, the night Hope saw the painting, bearing in mind she was more than a little drunk ... what if the woman in the painting then, was Hanna? Hanna dancing with you in the Great Hall on Christmas Eve. Hanna in your arms at The Mistletoe Dance. Hanna looking up into your eyes and you looking down at Hanna with all that love and desire and longing.'

'Yes. Thank you. I get the picture. Literally.' Now even Griff looked a little concerned. 'You're suggesting that Hanna painted that picture for herself, but then Hope spotted it and asked if she could give it to us as a present, so Hanna had no choice but to pretend the woman in her painting was you, and to alter it so that everyone else could see it was you?'

'Precisely. You see! Hanna is in love with you!'

Griff shook his head. 'I still find it hard to believe. And would Hanna really paint a life-size picture of herself dancing with me, knowing that someone else might see it? I know I'm irresistible and all that but ... Sorry. I shouldn't joke about it. And as I've said, it doesn't matter.' He reached out for her and she took his hand in hers. He gently pulled her back into his arms. 'I adore you, my darling. And only you. There will never be anyone else for me. Ever. Plus, I'm still not convinced about Hanna being in love with me. But there is one way to find out.'

'How?' Grace snuggled closer to him again and looked up into his dark eyes.

'We could ask Hanna.'

'Ask Hanna! Are you mad?' Grace pushed herself away and glared at Griff in disbelief.

'Erm. I'm mad about you,' he quipped.

'This is serious,' Grace snapped.

'No it's not, Grace. Because I'm sure it's not true. But why can't we ask Hanna? It seems to me that it's the sensible thing to do. It would clear this up in a minute.'

'We can't ask her because if she says it is true, we can't ignore it. At the moment this is simply gossip. We can pretend we haven't heard it yet. But if we ask her and she says it's true then she'll know that we know and we can't pretend we don't.'

'I see. I think.' He smiled lovingly. 'Can you pretend you haven't heard it, Grace? I can. But can you? I know you better than you might think I do and I'm fairly sure that you won't be able to. Of course, there is another option.'

He was right, obviously. Grace wouldn't be able to pretend for long. If at all. It would eat away at her until she blurted the question out herself and asked Hanna directly if she was in love with Griff.

'What's the other option?'

'We could ask Hope to ask her.'

Grace shook her head so vigorously it almost made her dizzy and the room spun for a second or two before she spoke.

'That's the same as me asking Hanna. Hanna will know that Hope will tell me. Even if Hanna swears Hope to secrecy.'

'Hmm. Okay. Then why don't we ask Russell to find out? Hanna knows he can be trusted with a secret. He's home for the Summer Fayre this weekend, so he's bound to bump into Hanna. He may be here already, because I'm sure I saw his car coming up the drive just before you said you needed to speak with me in private. They're friends. He's single. She's single. He could simply ask her if there is anyone she's interested in, romantically. He could even tell her he's heard a rumour that she's in love with me, and he could ask her if it's true. If Hanna really did tell Barbra Brimble that she's in love with me, then she'll have no qualms in telling Russell, will she? But if she was trying to keep it a secret and blurted it out by mistake, then she'll probably still admit that to him. He could say he knows what it's like to love someone who doesn't love you in return. What could be more natural? And if, as I believe we'll find will be the case, this is simply silly gossip and Hanna is not in love with me, then she'll be as horrified as you are, and she'll immediately tell Russell it isn't true.'

Grace couldn't argue with that.

Four

Hanna couldn't quite believe it, especially as the day had started off so well and had, if anything, only got better. Or so she thought. She'd even been able to dismiss the slight anxiety she had experienced after her irritating conversation with Barbra Brimble earlier. Her painting of Betancourt and its grounds was as beautiful as she had hoped, even allowing for the fact that she'd had to paint out that butterfly's long tail and she'd been looking forward to a small celebratory lunch at The Royal Oak.

She'd only nipped home to Catkin Cottage to put her easel and paints away and to wash her brushes thoroughly before leaving them to dry in a pretty, ceramic pot she kept in her studio specifically for that purpose.

If she'd known she might bump into Vera and Rita Boot, the elderly twin sisters who lived next door, she might have waited to return home. They were lovely, but they did have a tendency to talk, and talk, and talk, and she was feeling hungry. Her tummy had been rumbling like a worn out washing machine for the last half an hour. But they had spotted her the moment she had rounded the corner and it was obvious that, having seen her, they were now standing outside their front door, waiting for her. The eager waves and beckoning gestures had given that away.

Yet even after her earlier 'chat' with Barbra Brimble, and her misgivings about that, she was totally unprepared for what the sisters said. And she definitely hadn't expected them to feel sorry for her. Along with half of Betancourt Bay, apparently.

She could kick herself for being so foolish. And right now, she wouldn't mind giving Barbra Brimble a little kick too. Right off the top of Lookout Point. Or perhaps at the top of Lookout Steps. She could stand and watch Barbra Brimble's bottom bounce down all three hundred steps, one by one.

That made her smile for a second. Until the reality of what the Boot sisters were saying really dawned on her.

She only had herself to blame though. She was the one who had let out that long sigh in front of Barbra. She had said those stupid words aloud. And Barbra's radar dish like ears had honed in on them. The problem was, Barbra had entirely misunderstood what Hanna had said.

Well, maybe not entirely.

Now Hanna was facing a dilemma. Was it better to reveal her real secret and set the wagging tongues straight? Even though that might lead to more heartache. Or should she wait it out? But that might lead to more confusion and some very awkward questions.

And what about her friends, Griff and Grace? Had they heard this gossip yet?

Although would they care? Would they even believe it?

More importantly, would Russell?

The Boot sisters clearly had.

'How long have you been in love with Grifforde Betancourt, dear?' Rita had asked while Hanna was still a good few feet away.

The words had stopped Hanna in her tracks. It was a good thing that very few cars ever travelled along Oak Street, or she might have been knocked down. She couldn't move her feet for several seconds.

'Wh-what?' Hanna had thought she must have misheard Rita.

'In love with gorgeous Griff,' Vera had stated, letting out a rather loud and wistful sigh of her own. 'If only I were a few years younger. You'd have competition, dear.'

'Competition!' Rita shot her twin sister a withering look and snorted a laugh. 'Aren't you forgetting, young Grace? She's your competition for Griff's heart. And I'd also be in that line, let me tell you. That man is a hunk and there's no denying it.' She threw Hanna a sympathetic smile. 'We understand completely why you're in love with the man. I mean, who isn't? But what we don't understand, dear, is why you chose to tell Barbra. And why you waited until now. Surely it would've been better to declare how you felt before the man proposed to Grace, wouldn't it? Or better yet, before The Mistletoe Dance. Perhaps, if you'd got in first, he might not have told Grace how much he loved her.'

'They're not married yet though,' said Vera. 'And as we both know, there's many a hitch betwixt a proposal and the wedding vows.'

'We agreed we would never talk about that again!' Rita glowered at her sister, before hastily composing herself. 'We're trying to comfort Hanna, not dwell on the past. And really, Vera. Who uses the word 'betwixt' these days?'

Vera flushed slightly. 'Yes. Of course.' And then she smiled compassionately at Hanna. 'I suspect, like the rest of us, you had no idea how Grifforde felt about Grace until he declared himself on Christmas Eve. You probably thought, as we all did, that he was one of life's playboys, and that, one day, you might be the woman to tame him.'

'If only,' said Rita, rolling her eyes. 'But once he'd said he loved Grace, and had done so for most of his life, it didn't really matter when or how you admitted you loved him, did it? You must realise though, deep down, that it's too late.'

Vera tutted at her sister. 'What we mean is, was it wise to do so now? And do come out of the road, dear. Getting yourself run over won't help anyone.'

'Grace might disagree with that,' Rita said.

It was as if Hanna was in a trance until Rita's sarcasm snapped her out of it. She hurried to the pavement feeling more than a little foolish and annoyed.

'Are you ... are you honestly saying that Barbra has told you that I said I'm in love with Griff?'

'Oh no, dear,' said Vera, and Hanna breathed a sigh of relief. But it was short lived. 'Daisy Copeland called and told us.'

'Yes,' said Rita. 'We usually go to Daisy's Wednesday coffee mornings at the vicarage, but between you and us, ever since we invited Daisy and the vicar to our eightieth birthday party the man has been a little ... high and mighty towards us. He's often banging on about Genesis, and Sodom and Gomorrah, so we only go now when we know he won't be popping in.'

'He treats us as if we're little devils or something,' Vera said, giggling.

'Sorry.' Hanna was confused and her head was thumping. 'Are you telling me that the vicar's wife called you and said that I'm in love with Griff?'

'Yes, dear,' said Vera. 'About an hour ago now. Barbra Brimble was at the coffee morning, and she told Daisy, and everyone else present.'

Hanna briefly closed her eyes as the ground seemed to be shifting beneath her feet.

'Erm. How many people attend Daisy's coffee mornings?' Hanna dreaded the answer.

'Well it really depends,' said Rita, seemingly counting with her fingers as she spoke. 'At least half of the female residents of Betancourt Bay, I'd say.'

'Oh, great,' Hanna groaned.

'Oh no, dear,' said Vera, wagging a finger at her sister. 'Far more than that. I'd say most of the female residents of the village. At least, those above a certain age. And, of course, there are the members of St Gabriel's choir. Some of those live in Folkestone.'

'It just gets better,' Hanna mumbled as she shook her head.

'And the three female campanologists!' Rita seemed to suddenly remember, judging by her tone. 'Although why all the people who live in Folkestone come all the way here to our little church when there are some perfectly good churches in Folkestone, is a mystery to me.'

'St Gabriel's is pretty,' said Vera. 'And ancient.'

'We're pretty, and ancient,' Rita joked, 'but do people travel from Folkestone to come to us?'

'Well, yes dear.' Vera furrowed her brows. 'Our nephew does.'

'Other than Bruce, I meant,' snapped Rita.

'Okay. Thanks.' Hanna was close to snapping now. 'I think I get the picture.' She couldn't listen to much more of this. She had her answer.

Basically, a lot of people, both in Betancourt Bay, and beyond, believed she was in love with Grifforde Betancourt. The feeling in her tummy was no longer one of hunger, it was more like nausea now.

Vera tapped her on her arm. 'We were just on our way to meet Daisy for lunch in Betancourt Bay Café. And we'd better hurry as we're already late. We're here if you want to chat. Oh, and you're welcome to join us, dear.'

'Thanks. But no,' Hanna said, and watched as the sisters hurried away, their walking sticks tapping on the pavement in perfect rhythm.

Perhaps she should give lunch at The Royal Oak a miss and eat at home instead. Assuming she could actually eat anything at all after that conversation.

Barbra Brimble, and the vicar's wife, and at least half of Betancourt Bay, along with several people in Folkestone, thought she was in love with Griff. And no doubt every single one of those people had told at least one other person this astonishing news by now.

Daisy would definitely have told the vicar, who had doubtless said he would pray for Hanna, because that was his answer to everything.

And Hanna didn't doubt for a second that Charlie Tollard, the daughter of Freddie, the owner of The Royal Oak had heard this gossip, and that meant everyone in the pub would've heard it too. Charlie wasn't one for keeping secrets.

Hanna needed time to think. And time to decide what she should do next.

It was only as she opened the front door of Catkin Cottage and stepped inside that she realised something.

'Oh bloody hell!' She slammed the door shut behind her. 'I didn't say it wasn't true! I didn't even try to deny it.'

Well that was that. She was never venturing outside again.

Five

'You want me to do what?'

Russell had been enjoying the delicious lunch that Tabby had prepared, but now something seemed to be stuck in his throat and he gave a few small coughs to try to clear it. He hardly managed to get the words out.

'I know it sounds ridiculous,' Griff said, giving him an apologetic smile as Grace glowered at her fiancé. 'But my darling, Grace, is a little upset about it, and even though I've assured her it won't be true and it's just a bit of silly nonsense, it would set her mind at rest if we knew for sure.'

'I am here, you know,' Grace said, still glowering as she stuck her fork in a carrot in a particularly ferocious manner, making both Griff and Russell wince. 'And what if it's not "just a bit of silly nonsense" and it's actually true?' She pulled a face as she mimicked Griff.

Russell grinned for a second. 'That

sounded almost like you, Griff,' he teased. Then he shook his head. He'd been astonished by the gossip when Tabby had told him about it, and even he had wondered if there might be some truth in it. But the more he thought about it the less he believed it. He'd seen Hanna and Griff together several times and not once did she give the appearance of a woman in love with his brother. She didn't look at Griff the way Grace looked at him. Or the way Hope looked at Tom. But he didn't want to go there. 'It's nonsense, Grace. I agree with Griff. But it's not silly. It's unkind to Hanna, and it's clearly hurtful to you.'

'And what about me?' Griff said. Now it was his turn to pull a face.

Russell raised an eyebrow. 'As if you care.'

'Stop joking about this, Griff!' Grace snapped, slapping him on the arm. 'I keep telling you, this isn't funny. At least Russell agrees with me on that score.'

'I'm sorry, darling,' Griff said, capturing her hand in his and kissing it. 'I know it's not funny and I apologise for trying to make light of it. But I'm not sure what else to do. I do care though. I care that it bothers you so much. And now I care about Hanna. I hadn't considered that she might be upset by this too. I assumed she'd simply see the funny side of it.'

'As you do,' Grace said.

'Well, yes. I'm sure there's a simple explanation and this is all a misunderstanding.'

Russell frowned. 'Why don't you simply ask Hanna?'

Griff rolled his eyes. 'Grace doesn't want Hanna to know we've heard this little titbit. Just in case it's true. This way we can pretend we know nothing about the gossip, and carry on as normal. Except, of course, we can't, because Grace is upset. As am I, obviously,' Griff hastily added.

'So you want me to ask Hanna if she's in love with you, Griff, and to assure her I won't say a word to either you or Grace, is that correct? And then, once I know for certain, to come and tell you both?'

Griff and Grace exchanged glances and nodded. 'Yes.'

'Isn't that lying? Not to mention, betraying Hanna's trust.'

'It is,' said Griff. 'But I see no other way around it.'

'Can't you merely ignore it? If Hanna is in love with you, surely you'd be able to tell, wouldn't you?'

Griff sighed and leant back in his chair. 'Grace and I have already had this conversation, and we're going around in circles. Will you help us, or not?'

Russell shot a look at Grace. She was usually so full of life and so happy whenever he saw her. Now she looked drawn and anxious.

Even Griff, who rarely took anything seriously unless he had to, appeared a little tense. Griff always tried to find a light in any darkness, but the woman he adored was upset and it seemed that for once in his life, Griff didn't know how to handle this turn of events.

Actually, for the second time in his life. Griff hadn't coped well when their mother had passed away. But then neither had Russell or their father.

'Of course I'll help you,' Russell said. 'Although I'll have to find a way to bring this up with Hanna. I can't go knocking on her door and asking her outright, can I? That would be incredibly rude.'

'And yet you suggested we should do so,' Griff reminded him, with a hint of sarcasm in his tone.

'Because you and Grace are directly involved. You both have a right to ask. Especially you, Griff. But if I ask, it just makes me nosy and Hanna would have every right to tell me to mind my own business. Leave it with me. I'll think of something.'

But having thought about it over lunch,

and then during coffee, and later, while basking in the sunshine and drinking another bottle of beer in the garden that afternoon, knocking on Hanna's door seemed precisely what he should do.

And there was no time like the present.

Six

Hanna had taken a while to decide whether or not to open her front door, but whoever was knocking on it was persistent and clearly had no intention of going away.

The last person she expected to find standing on the doorstep of Catkin Cottage though, was Russell Betancourt.

'Hello, Hanna. How are you? I hope I'm not disturbing you.'

Hanna felt her mouth drop open, and she wouldn't have been at all surprised if her eyes had popped out of her head on stalks, like they did in cartoons. Her voice seemed to have disappeared and for a moment or two all she could do was shake her head and stare at him.

'Hi, Russell,' she eventually managed, her voice little more than a squeak. And then she regained a modicum of self control and added, 'I'm fine, thanks, and no. You're not disturbing me.'

That couldn't be farther from the truth. No one disturbed her more than Russell Betancourt did these days. Especially when he smiled that dazzling smile of his which always seemed to light up his deep blue eyes, and when the sunlight brought out the flecks of almost ice-white in his golden blond hair as it was doing right now.

She wasn't sure why, or even how, she had fallen in love with Russell, but the realisation, when it hit her, had come as a complete surprise.

It had happened at Easter, during the Grand Opening of Betancourt Bay Café, and she was still coming to terms with it, if she were being honest.

Until then, Russell had simply been Russell. The younger brother of Griff Betancourt, and just like his older brother, the perfect gentleman.

But he was also the man who had been in love with her friend, Hope Eversley, and had made a bit of a fool of himself by telling Hope how he felt, on Christmas Eve. The man who had been the focus of village gossips for weeks on end, and had been spending most of his time in London since Hope had met and fallen in love with her new boyfriend, Tom. No doubt because he couldn't bear to be in the same village as the woman he loved, knowing she would never feel the same way about him.

Hanna was beginning to understand how that might feel, although, luckily for her, Russell was hardly ever in Betancourt Bay these days.

In fact, she hadn't seen him since Easter. Moments after her epiphany. She had been sitting beside him when realisation dawned.

They, along with all the residents of Betancourt Bay, and some holidaymakers, were watching Griff cut the bright blue ribbon pinned across the new, glass, double front doors of Betancourt Bay Café.

Hanna had been at the edge of the throng, because she had been running late and had only just made it in time to hear Griff's speech, and Russell had appeared from nowhere and had come and stood beside her.

Griff had made a short and amusing speech and was wishing Naomi Hart, and her boyfriend, Lucas Dove, the best of everything in their business venture and their lives together.

'I don't think I need to wish you Good Luck, Naomi,' Griff had said. 'You've won the Lottery Jackpot, so luck is definitely on your side. But I do wish you the best of everything that life can bring you. Good health, even greater wealth, and true happiness for both you and Lucas. This café has been here for many years but you have transformed it from a place people rarely wanted to visit, into what I am certain will be the hub of village life. Together with The Royal Oak, and St Gabriel's Church, of course,' he added hastily. 'May you be exceedingly happy in your new home, and extraordinarily successful in your new business.' With that, Griff had cut the ribbon, and everyone had cheered.

'Finally,' Russell had joked, when trays loaded with glasses of champagne had appeared while everyone was clapping. 'I've only come for this.'

He had taken two glasses and handed one to Hanna, and it had struck her that he was a perfect gentleman. He could've simply taken one for himself and let her get her own, and yet he hadn't.

And when Naomi had thanked Griff profusely, and then announced that everyone should help themselves to food, and the row of tables outside, where platters of delicious looking buffet fare were drawing crowds, Russell had asked Hanna if he could get her something to eat.

She had thought it might be his way of excusing himself, and that he was really going off to mingle with others, but not only had he returned minutes later with a plate of food for her, he'd also brought a plate of food for Malorie Blackwell, another resident of the village who had come to chat with Hanna.

That meant he must have glanced back at Hanna and noticed that Malorie had joined her.

And that had got Hanna thinking.

Why had Russell come and stood beside her, of all people?

Was it because he had seen she was alone and had thought she might need some company?

But if so, then why had he looked back at her whilst filling their plates?

And why, having rejoined her, had he remained where he was, and not walked away now that she had someone else to talk to?

And when Malorie had moved on, and Griff had asked Russell if he would help him and Lucas move some more tables and chairs outside now that it looked as if the sunshine would prevail, why had Russell seemed a little disappointed?

He had turned to her and smiled that dazzling smile and said, 'Don't run away, will you?'

And she hadn't.

She had stayed precisely where she was, even when Hope and Tom had come over and chatted and invited her to join the rest of the Eversley family who were seated at one of the many additional tables now being provided.

'I've been sitting at my easel all morning,' she had said. 'It's good to stand for a while.'

'Then come and stand near us,' Hope had coaxed.

'Maybe in a minute,' she had said. 'Malorie said she'll be coming back and she'll think I'm being rude if I'm not here.'

Why had she lied to Hope and Tom?

Was she being foolish?

Was she imagining things?

Russell was still in love with Hope, wasn't he?

And if he had got over Hope, would he really be interested in Hanna?

Of course he wouldn't.

And even if he were, was she interested in him?

Russell had returned shortly after with that gorgeous smile still in place, the sleeves of his white shirt rolled up, and his grey linen jacket slung over one broad shoulder. He carried two fold up chairs in one hand, and a fold up table in the other, and had asked if she would like to sit.

'I'd love to,' she had replied, with just the merest glance in Hope's direction.

They had chatted and laughed for what seemed like just a few minutes but in reality was almost an hour, and then, all too soon, Griff and Grace had come to join them, and the rest of the afternoon had flown.

Griff and Grace had finally left, and were walking away hand in hand and staring into one another's eyes, and Russell had said, somewhat wistfully, 'I can only imagine what it must feel like being as in love as those two are.'

Hanna had assumed he must be thinking about Hope and wishing that he and Hope could've been like Griff and Grace.

And that's when Hanna had had her epiphany.

She had looked at Russell as a slight breeze had lifted strands of his golden blond hair away from his left temple, and she had found herself wishing that he might look at her the way Griff looked at Grace.

It had taken her so much by surprise that she had sat bolt upright, mumbled something inaudible about not being able to choose with whom she fell in love, and had thankfully been rescued by none other than Hope herself who had come back, this time alone, to ask Hanna about one of her paintings that Tom had spotted hanging in The Royal Oak.

'Sorry to barge in,' Hope had said, looking a little awkward as she had glanced at Russell, 'but I wanted to ask if you might be free later, Hanna, when this has finished. Tom's seen a painting of yours in the pub, and he absolutely loves it. I wondered if you might have something similar in your studio. Or if not, whether you might paint something like it? I want to give it to him as a surprise gift.'

'Erm. Of course. Yes,' said Hanna, needing to get away from Russell before she said something stupid. 'I was just thinking it's time I left, so I'm free now, if you are.'

She stood up so fast her chair fell over.

Russell stood up too, like the perfect gentleman he was.

'You're leaving?' he asked, looking her in the eye before bending down and picking up the chair.

'It's late,' Hanna said, even though it wasn't. 'Erm. I have things I need to do. Sorry. But thank you for a lovely afternoon. I've ... I've really enjoyed it.'

'Me too,' said Russell. 'Thank you for your company.'

He gave an odd little bow as he stood there, smiling. Although the smile seemed a little less dazzling.

'If you're busy,' Hope said, 'we can do it another time.'

'No!' Hanna shrieked. 'Erm. Now is fine. Goodbye Russell.'

That was the day she had realised she

was head over heels in love with Russell Betancourt.

And that was the last time she had seen him.

Until now.

That dazzling smile firmly in place as he stood right in front of her on the doorstep of Catkin Cottage.

Seven

Russell wasn't sure what to do next. Hanna seemed to be in a world of her own. He had been standing on her doorstep for what felt like an eternity, a smile fixed firmly in place, and yet she hadn't invited him in.

'Erm. I can come back later if this isn't a good time,' he said.

'Good time?' She was definitely flustered. 'For what?'

'To have a chat with you. Erm. I've come home for the Summer Fayre this weekend. And I realised that the last time I saw you was when I was home at Easter. For the Grand Opening of Betancourt Bay Café. Erm. I was on my way to the pub. No. The café. Erm. I was out for a walk and I found myself in Oak Street. So I thought, why not go and say hello to Hanna Shaw. She lives on Oak Street. So here I am. To say hello.'

'Hell-o,' she repeated, giving him the strangest look imaginable.

But then she would, wouldn't she? He was behaving like a complete buffoon.

What on earth was wrong with him?

He'd felt perfectly in control until she had opened the front door. He'd managed to get out the few sentences he'd repeated over and over again on his way here, without any trouble. He'd even been able to say a few more things that sounded reasonably sensible.

But now ... well, now ... he didn't seem to be in complete control of his faculties.

When Tabby had first mentioned Hanna earlier that day and had told him about the gossip, he had been shocked as well as surprised.

But he hadn't thought about why he was so shocked and so surprised.

Even during lunch, when he and Griff and Grace were discussing it, he hadn't let himself wonder why there was a tightness in his chest. Or why he was a little annoyed about the gossip. He, like Griff, had tried to make light of it.

As if Hanna would be in love with Griff! It was ridiculous.

But was it?

Lots of women were in love with Griff. Griff was the epitome of tall, dark, and handsome. Women sometimes literally swooned when Griff bestowed one of his intense gazes and sensational smiles on them.

Yet Hanna had never seemed that interested.

Or had she?

The truth was, until this year, Russell had hardly noticed Hanna because he had been so in love with Hope.

He had thought Hanna was pretty when they had first met, a few years ago now, when she had moved to Betancourt Bay. He had known she was a talented artist. Both he and Griff had bought her paintings. And she had always been easy to talk to whenever they had seen one another. But other than that, he had given Hanna very little thought.

And yet, since Christmas, he had thought of Hanna once or twice. A few times, in fact. Since Griff and Grace's engagement in February, he had thought of Hanna far more often than he had thought of Hope. And since Easter, he had hardly thought of Hope at all, yet thoughts of Hanna had frequently popped into his head, and he had found himself smiling, yet he wasn't sure why.

They were merely friends, and he had enjoyed his time with her that day at the Grand Opening of Betancourt Bay Café.

He had been disappointed not to have come home in June. Yet he had also been slightly relieved that he could stay away. He wasn't sure what was happening to him but he had felt a change somehow. He couldn't put his finger on it but something was different. There was one thing he was certain of though. He was no longer in love with Hope Eversley.

Even during his chat with Tabby today, and then the conversation with Griff and Grace he hadn't understood why this latest gossip was playing on his mind. It didn't involve him in any way, other than the fact that he was Griff's younger brother.

But was that all it was? Why did it make him cross to think that everyone was spreading gossip about Hanna? And was it simply the gossip that was irritating him? Or was there something more?

It was only as he walked down the drive of Betancourt and crossed the road into Oak Street that light seemed to dawn. And when he had seen Catkin Cottage a surge of excitement had grown inside him. His footsteps had quickened and he had felt light headed as soon as he had seen Hanna's front door.

And as he had stood on her doorstep and she had opened the door to him, all he could think about was how pleased he was to see her again.

And now all he could think about was

how beautiful she was, with her hair tied in a sort of loosely tangled bun, and how the yellow T-shirt she was wearing showed off every curve to perfection. How her cropped pale blue jeans clung to her long and shapely legs.

Did her tan go all the way from the tips of her bare feet to the outline of her gloriously lustrous auburn hair?

Was it an all over body tan or were there patches of soft white skin outlined in the shape of a swimsuit? Or of a skimpy bikini, perhaps?

Was her skin as silky smooth as he imagined it would be?

And when, exactly, had he started imagining how silky smooth her skin might be?

Pull yourself together man, he silently reprimanded himself as his eyes met hers and she quickly looked away.

'Actually,' she mumbled, standing awkwardly on one leg now while the other leg appeared to be slowly turning away from him as if she were intending to run. 'This isn't a good time to chat. I … I need to finish washing out my brushes. And I need to change. Plus I … I've got a lot to do. I'll see you at the Summer Fayre. Erm. Thanks for calling round though. Bye.'

She shut the door so fast it almost hit

him on the nose.

He stood and looked at the paintwork, too close for comfort, and then he shook his head and stepped onto the pavement.

'Smooth, Russell. Really smooth. The pub and the café are both in the other direction, you idiot. What is wrong with you?'

And then he felt as if that door had hit him, because a sudden realisation had.

He had come here today on behalf of Griff and Grace to find a way to ask Hanna if the rumours and the gossip were true and whether she was in love with Griff.

But although they had asked him to come here, the reason he *was* here, was for himself. He needed to know the answer because there was no way that he could do that whole unrequited love thing all over again.

And yet, even if Hanna told him that she was in love with Griff, Russell knew that somehow he would find a way to ask her the question he had just realised he really wanted to ask.

Which was whether there was even the remotest chance that she might consider going out on a date with him.

Huh! So much for being unable to do that unrequited love thing again.

Eight

Grace couldn't blame Russell. Hanna had said she was too busy to talk and had closed her front door before he'd had a chance to say much at all. He couldn't exactly kick it down and demand an answer, could he? No matter how much Grace wanted to know whether the gossip was true or not.

But Grace had a strange feeling that Russell hadn't told her and Griff everything, and he seemed a little more irritable than he had before he had gone out for a walk.

He hadn't even told them he was going to visit Hanna, and all he said when he returned was that he'd knocked on her door as he'd been passing, but that she was busy, and had closed the door before he'd had a chance to talk to her, adding that he'd call back another time.

'So what's the plan now then?' Hope asked, after Grace had explained the current situation to her, and the rest of the Eversley family the following day.

They were seated around the large, circular, pine table in the kitchen of The White House, the heart of the Eversley home, holding one of their usual morning meetings to discuss the family business, Eversley Events.

The biggest and most important event scheduled in the business diary was, of course, Grace's wedding, which was now just a little over two weeks away, on Saturday the 24th of August. Every member of the family was extremely excited about that.

Even Granny Joy, Pat Eversley's mum, although she was currently snoring in her armchair and had been since before Grace and Hope had arrived at just after nine a.m. making enough noise between them to wake the dead, although not, apparently, Granny Joy.

Alongside her was Lady Elizabeth, the family's French Bulldog, who was curled up fast asleep in her basket beside the large green Aga, next to her water bowl. Her stubby nose and her big 'bat ears' were twitching as she slept; she was no doubt dreaming of juicy bones, or special, doggy treats, and probably not of Grace's wedding.

Grace, Hope, Pat, and Simon Eversley were drinking coffee and eating freshly baked croissants that Hope had brought with her from a bakery in Folkestone which was close to the house her boyfriend Tom was currently renting where Hope had spent the night, as she so often did these days.

'I have no idea,' said Grace, as she pulled her croissant into tiny pieces. 'Griff and Russell both think we should all carry on as if nothing has changed. And annoyingly, so does Tabby.'

'What does Archie think?' Simon asked.

'Their dad thinks the same. Just as I know you and Mum do, Dad. But it's not as simple as that. Hanna is my friend. Or she's supposed to be. She should be coming out with us on my hen night, but now I don't know what to do. It's only ten days away, and what if it's true that she's in love with Griff? Won't that be awkward?'

'To say the least,' said Hope. 'I still say you should ask her if it's true. If it's not, then you have nothing to worry about and you can stop fretting over it. If it is, well, then you can politely suggest she doesn't attend the hen night. Or, more importantly, the wedding. The last thing you want is for the vicar to ask if anyone has any reason why you and Griff shouldn't be married, and for Hanna to stand on a pew in St Gabriel's church and shout, 'It should be me!' or something equally dramatic.'

Grace gulped in a breath. 'Do you think

she might do that?'

Hope shrugged. 'Who knows? People do all sorts of silly things when they're in love.'

Pat tutted. 'Of course she won't. Hanna isn't that sort of person. She's not a drama Queen. If this gossip is true – which I seriously doubt – I think Hanna is more likely to have a quiet word with Griff before the wedding.'

'Have a quiet word with Griff!' Grace repeated in a shrill voice. 'What does that mean?'

Hope snorted derisively. 'That she'll ask him if he wants to change his mind, and marry her instead.'

'That's not what I meant at all,' said Pat, throwing Hope a quelling look. 'I meant, she might tell Griff how she feels and explain that she needs to keep her distance. And I was going to add that she would probably also have a word with me, and say that she would rather not be a guest at the wedding.'

'Surely it's me she should be talking to?' Grace moaned.

'She's probably feeling embarrassed,' said Pat. 'If it's true. Which it's not. And if it's not true, she's probably mortified that the entire village seems to think it is. Apart from all of us, of course. And Griff and his family, too. I've told everyone who's mentioned it to me that I'm sure it's all just silly nonsense and that they should ignore it and stop gossiping about it.'

Hope grinned. 'And how's that working out for you, Mum? Even Tom's sister has heard it, and she and her fiancée, Alice both live in Folkestone. They came over to Tom's for dinner last night and Della asked me if I knew about it, and whether it was true. Obviously, I said it wasn't and that we were treating it with the contempt it deserved.'

'Thank you,' said Grace. 'The thing I don't understand though is, if it isn't true, why didn't Hanna come and talk to me the moment the gossip started spreading? Surely, if there's a simple explanation, as Griff and all of you keep telling me there is, she would've come and explained it to me, wouldn't she?'

'Why?' Granny Joy piped up, making everyone at the table jump. 'Friendship goes both ways, you know, Grace. Perhaps it didn't occur to Hanna that you might believe it. Maybe she assumed you and Griff would dismiss it as nonsense. She might've thought that mentioning it to you might, in some strange way, give the gossip some sort of credence. Or maybe it is true and she thinks the best thing to do is to stay out of the way and not say a word about it. The Royal Family doesn't pay any attention to gossip, Grace, and neither should you. Carrying on like some sort of petulant child will only give the gossips fuel for their fire. And that's the last thing you should do.'

'Petulant child! I'm doing no such thing. But I think I have a right to know if a friend of mine is in love with my fiancé!'

'Why? Will it make him love you any less? Are you worried he might run off with Hanna and leave you at the altar?'

'Of course not!'

'Then I really don't see why you have a problem. If Hanna loves Griff, she's the one with the problem, not you. And she can still be your friend even if she does love Griff. Russell loved Hope but did it make him some sort of monster? Did we bar him from the door? No. We all let him be, and remained friendly, and now he's over her. Perhaps what Hanna needs is your understanding and, possibly, a bit of compassion. Love can take us all by surprise. Forget about the gossip, and make me a nice cup of coffee. Are those croissants you're eating? I hope you've left one for me.'

Nine

Russell read the text again, and smiled, before slipping his phone into the pocket of the jacket slung over his other arm. Then he called out 'Goodbye' to Tabby and headed towards the double front doors.

It was a gloriously sunny morning and excitement bubbled inside him, like it had when he was a youngster going out on a day trip with his family. But this was no family day out. This was a day out with Hanna, and he still couldn't quite believe it was happening.

After the debacle of his visit yesterday, he wasn't sure what to do next, and then a thought had struck him as he had sat in the garden last evening, watching a stunningly beautiful sunset and listening to the crickets chirping in the grass, and the birds twittering in the branches of the trees. The sky reminded him of a painting of Hanna's he had seen in the pub, and that, in turn, reminded him of another friend of his.

He immediately sent Hanna a text. A rather long text.

'I know you're busy, but if you fancy a change of scene tomorrow, I'm off to Hastings for the day. A friend of mine from uni, has opened an art gallery in the Old Town and I keep promising I'll pop in. She's a massive fan of your artwork and she'd love to meet you. Plus, I could use the company on the drive. Ping me a text if you're interested, but no problem if you're not. Although I'd score a lot of bonus points as a friend if I turned up with you by my side, so you'd be doing me a favour, and you'd have a lovely day out. I'll buy you lunch. And possibly, an ice cream.'

He'd signed off with his name. No emojis, no kisses, no endearments. He'd hoped the text was friendly and light-hearted.

He'd checked his phone every five minutes, but she hadn't replied before he'd joined Grace, Griff, and Archie for dinner. Phones weren't allowed at the table in the evening but he'd checked his again the moment he'd gone into the sitting room for coffee. Still no reply.

He'd given up hope by the time he went to bed.

But at five past eight this morning, as

he'd stepped out of the shower, the ping of a text message made him dash to his phone, his wet feet almost making him slip on the tiled floor of his en suite.

And there it was. The text he'd been waiting for.

'Sorry for the delay. I'd love to join you if the offer's still there.'

He'd sent an immediate reply.

'I'll pick you up at nine-thirty. See you soon.'

He'd spent longer than usual deciding what to wear and had finally settled on casual dark grey trousers, a dark grey polo shirt and his light grey linen jacket. Black leather loafers completed his ensemble and he gave himself a quick once-over in the full-length mirror before racing off to breakfast. Tabby had often told him that dark grey brought out the blue of his eyes, and he'd laughed at himself as he trotted down the stairs. He had never been one to worry too much about his clothing, and yet, somehow, today it mattered to him.

Grace was having a breakfast meeting with her own family, so luckily she wasn't at breakfast to ask him awkward questions, and for some reason he decided not to tell Griff or Archie, that Hanna would be joining him on his jaunt to Hastings.

'You're looking pleased with yourself,'

his father had noticed as Russell marched into the dining room. 'Going somewhere special?'

'No. Just to see an old friend.' He'd slung his jacket over the chair beside him and spotted the grin on Griff's mouth. 'In Hastings,' he'd added.

'Emma?' Griff raised his brows. 'Today?'

'Why not? I've been promising to pop in for a while, and it looks like the perfect day for a drive. I'm not needed here, am I?'

Griff shook his head. 'No. Everything's under control. The marquees won't be arriving until tomorrow and we've got the usual team to set those up. Grace and her family have kindly given us a hand this year, and Tabby's given Grace some pointers, so the catering should be better than ever at this year's Summer Fayre. All we need now is good weather this weekend.'

No one mentioned the gossip, and Russell was glad of that. If Grace had been there, it might've been a different story.

'Enjoy your day out,' Archie said, glancing up from the newspaper he'd been reading, when Russell stood up to depart.

'Yes,' said Griff, grinning yet again, almost as if he knew exactly what Russell had planned. 'I hope it is the perfect day ... for your drive.'

'Thanks. I hope you both have a good day

too.'

After breakfast, and calling out Goodbye to Tabby, Russell hurried to his car, and seconds later, roared down the drive of Betancourt, then crossed into Oak Street and in less than one minute had pulled up outside Catkin Cottage.

He leapt out of his car, knocked on her door, and a moment later they were standing face to face. Well, almost face to face. He was a good six inches taller, and, unless he was mistaken, she was trying to avoid looking up into his eyes by bending her head.

He took the opportunity to admire her from head to toe. Her hair was loose but even he could see she must've spent time getting the ends to curl under so perfectly. Her make up was barely visible, but was there. Her eyes were emphasised by the mascara on her long lashes, and her lips gleamed a cherry red, which matched the polish on the nails of her fingers and toes. The fitted yellow dress, almost the same yellow as the T-shirt she'd worn yesterday, highlighted her curves, and the hemline being at least four inches above her knees made her tanned and shapely legs look even longer.

'It's a beautiful day,' he said, his throat feeling slightly croaky, 'and you look lovely. Erm. Unless you'd rather we didn't, I thought we'd have the top down.' He pointed towards his convertible. 'I don't want to spoil your hair though.'

Now she did smile up at him. 'I'd love that. And don't worry about my hair. I can tie it back.' She searched in her handbag for a few seconds and pulled out a colourful, elasticated hairband. 'Scrunchie!'

'Isn't that a chocolate covered honeycomb bar?' he quipped.

'Now you've made me want a Crunchie.' She carefully smoothed her hair into a loose knot. 'Better yet. A Crunchie ice cream.'

'At this time in the morning?'

'Any time is perfect for ice cream.' She stepped out and closed her front door. 'Is this a new car?'

He nodded. 'Yes. The last time I had a soft top was in my late teens. A friend who owns a dealership persuaded me it was time I had another. I may have had a couple of glasses of whisky when we had that conversation.'

She grinned at him as he held the passenger door open for her. 'The last time I was in a convertible, it chucked it down, and the top got stuck open. We were drenched by the time we got home.'

'And you're willing to give it another go?' He laughed as she nodded, and he closed the door. Then, once in the driver's seat, he pressed the button to make the roof close and reopen again. 'Seems to be working so far. But I do have an umbrella in the boot if things go wrong.'

'Good to know,' she said, as he pressed the start button.

He drove back the way he'd come, turning right out of Oak Street and onto Folkestone Road.

'It should take us about an hour,' he said. 'I thought we'd avoid the motorway and take the scenic route. Would you like to listen to some music?'

'No. Unless you want to.'

'Nope. I'm happy to chat. Or to just enjoy the scenery.'

'Same here,' she replied, and they travelled in silence for a few minutes as he made his way through the outskirts of Folkestone and onto the road towards Hastings. 'So ... this friend of yours is from your days at uni?'

'Yes. We've kept in touch but we don't see one another often. I see her twin brother more frequently. He lives in London, so we have lunch from time to time. Or we'll meet for a game of squash.'

'I didn't know you played squash.'

'I expect there're a few things you don't know about me. What about you? Do you play any sports?'

'Tennis. But not often. I played netball at

school. I've never played squash.'

'I'm happy to give you a lesson if you want to try it. Folkestone has some good squash courts.'

'I'd like that. Thanks. It's always good to try new things. Do you play tennis?'

'I do. Perhaps we could have a game of that as well.'

'Yes. That might be fun. So what else don't I know about you?'

He shot her a glance, and grinned. 'That's difficult to say because unless I know what you do know about me it's difficult to know what you don't.'

'True. I know you're a perfect gentleman. I know what you do, who all the members of your family are, and where you live. I know you have long term friendships, as we're going to see a friend you've known for years, and I also know you're still friends with all the people who were kids in the village at the same time as you. I know you keep your promises, because you said in your text that you promised you'd pop in to see this friend's art gallery. Oh! I know you like art. Because you've bought several of my paintings. I also know you're a good dancer. I remember that from The Mistletoe Dance. And I know you're loyal and ... Erm.'

'Yes?' he asked as her voice trailed off.

She shook her head and lowered her

gaze. 'Nothing. That's ... that's all I can think of, for now.'

'Were you going to say that you knew I had been in love with someone who didn't love me in return? Because it's okay, if you were. I did love Hope, I'll admit that. But I'm completely over her now.'

Hanna's head shot up. 'Completely?'

'Yes, Hanna. Completely. I still like her, obviously, and I think we'll always be friends. We've been friends since we were kids, as you said. But I can honestly say I don't love her anymore.'

'That's good. Erm. For you, I mean.'

'Yes. It is. So what about you? Is there someone you've got your eye on?'

'Me! No! Why do you ask?'

'Sorry. I didn't mean to upset you.'

'I'm not upset. I'm...' She stared at him. 'Wait a minute. Is that ... is that what this day trip is about? Have you heard something, Russell? Something concerning me? Something Barbra Brimble might have said?'

He shot her a sideways glance. Their conversation had flowed so freely and easily and he hadn't even thought about what he was saying.

'That wasn't why I asked. It really wasn't. But I won't lie to you, Hanna. Yes. I have heard some gossip. But I don't take any notice of things people say, and I don't judge people because I have no right to do so. I will say this though. I know how it feels to have everyone in the village talking about you behind your back. And whether or not there's any truth in what they say, it's hurtful. I'm a friend, Hanna. And I'd really like you to think of me as someone you can talk to, about anything. Anything at all. I'm here for you, if you need me. And I'm here for you if you don't. Let's leave it at that for now, and change the subject, shall we? I don't want to spoil this day.'

Hanna didn't say a word but she nodded very slowly, and then she looked in the other direction and watched the scenery whizz by.

Ten

Hanna took several deep breaths and stared at the scenery, which was a total blur right now. It had been such a lovely start to their day out and now it had turned into a disaster. Should she ask him to drop her at a station so that she could get a train back to Folkestone, and a cab back to Betancourt Bay? She couldn't spend the day with him after this.

And yet. He hadn't said anything about Griff. Or about her being in love with someone else's fiancé. But if he'd heard the gossip then he must've known what it was about.

He knew better than anyone how unrequited love felt, so was he telling her he understood how she was feeling? And was he also telling her that he was willing to help her if he could? He'd said that he was a friend. He'd said he wanted her to talk to him about anything at all. He also said he was there for her if she needed him. And even if she didn't, he would still be there. What did that mean, exactly?

Did it mean that he was offering to help her through this? To help her get over what he thought was her unrequited love for Griff? And how, precisely, would he do that?

By talking with her? By spending time with her? By giving the gossips something else to talk about? Because if they knew Hanna and Russell were out together today, tongues would soon start wagging.

Was that so bad? People already thought she was in love with Griff. Did it matter if they started wondering why she was spending time with Russell?

The only thing that did matter of course, was that Russell couldn't find out what her true secret was. If he knew that it wasn't Griff she was in love with, but Russell himself, would he run a mile? Would she ever see him again? Would he avoid her at all costs?

She wasn't sure what she should do.

She watched him surreptitiously, her head lowered and half turned away.

Whatever she chose to do, he would never be unkind.

And everyone thought she was in love with Griff, so what harm was there in pretending it was true?

Grace knew how much Griff loved her so

she wouldn't care about the gossip. She probably wouldn't believe it anyway. She must've heard it by now, and if it had concerned her, wouldn't she have called and asked Hanna if there was any truth in it? Hanna would tell her soon. But not too soon. Grace, and her sister Hope, weren't good at keeping secrets. If Grace knew Hanna was in love with Russell, she would instantly tell Griff, and probably Russell too.

Being able to spend some time with Russell would be worth the lie, wouldn't it? Because that seemed to be what Russell was offering. But he wouldn't offer that if she told him he was the one she was in love with. Or if Grace, or Hope, or anyone else blurted it out.

When a lie might bring her closer to her secret wish, and the truth might tear her apart, choosing the right path wasn't easy.

Eleven

The morning was growing hotter and the sun beat down as Russell and Hanna sat in a queue of traffic. They had driven in silence for the last ten or fifteen minutes, partly because Russell wasn't sure if Hanna had dozed off, or if she was simply ignoring him, and partly because he couldn't think of the right thing to say after their earlier conversation. But now he had to say something.

'Would you like me to pull over somewhere so that we can get that ice cream? It shouldn't be much longer, once we get out of this traffic jam, but it's already a scorcher. Shall I put the roof up and turn on the air conditioning?'

'I don't mind,' she said, without turning to look at him. 'I'm fine. But if you want the roof up, that's also fine with me. And I can wait for the ice cream. Good things are worth waiting for, so I've heard.' Now she did give him a brief smile, and relief surged through him.

'I'm fine too. Erm. Have you been to Hastings before?'

'Nope. I've heard of it, of course. Who hasn't? The Battle in 1066. The arrow in King Harold's eye. The Bayeux Tapestry. William the Conqueror, and all that. But no. I've never been there. Have you?'

'No. It'll be an adventure for both of us. I hear there's a Crazy Golf course on the seafront.' He grinned across at her. 'And, of course, like Folkestone, the town is famous for its fishing fleet. There're caves in the cliffs, where smugglers hid their goods in a maze of tunnels. There're a couple of museums. And all the usual things a seaside town has to offer.'

'Like deckchairs you trap your fingers in, and seagulls pooing on your head and nicking your chips, you mean?'

'Yes. Exactly like that. Which is why we'll eat at a restaurant.'

'I'm glad you're paying then.'

He threw her a smile. 'Ah, at last. The traffic is moving again. Hastings, here we come.'

'I bet that's what William the Conqueror said,' she joked. 'Although I suppose he came by boat.'

'And he didn't land in Hastings. He

landed a little farther along the coast, although from what I read on line, there's some dispute as to the precise location. Plus, the battle wasn't in Hastings either. It was at Senlac Hill, a few miles north of Hastings, and where the town of Battle is now situated.'

'It must've been a tough life in those days. I bet they didn't have ice cream either.'

'No. It makes you wonder how they survived.'

Their banter seemed to be back on track and they chatted amiably for the rest of the journey to the Old Town of Hastings.

'Is it actually called 'the Old Town' and is that because there's a new town?' Hanna asked as they neared their destination.

'Yes. And there's the sign to prove it. That coat of arms on the sign is the heraldic emblem of the Cinque Ports, and Hastings is one of the original towns. Since those first five towns of Hastings, Romney, Hythe, Dover, and Sandwich, were given the status, other towns, like Folkestone, have been added, as so called, limbs, of the originals.'

'Why are there three golden lions, cut in half and attached to the sterns of three gold ships? Is that depicting the lions of England, and the ships providing service to the Crown?'

'That's exactly what it is.'

'I'm not just a pretty face and a hugely

talented artist,' she joked. 'I can also read stuff in books and on the internet.'

Russell laughed. 'I knew that.'

He parked in the car park at a place called The Stade at one end of the Old Town and bought them both an ice cream as they wandered along the promenade. They strolled past the fun fair and the boating lake, until they reached the Crazy Golf course where Hanna challenged him to a game. Which she won.

From there they walked along George Street which was pedestrianised, and they popped in and out of a variety of shops until Hanna announced she was starving.

They found a restaurant that served fresh fish, and had a covered outside space, providing the best of both worlds. They were shaded from the glare of the sun but could still sit outside and watch the world go by.

After lunch they visited the art gallery Russell's friend from uni had opened.

'This is Emma,' Russell said, introducing his friend to Hanna. 'And Emma, this is Hanna, a good friend of mine from Betancourt Bay.'

Emma shrieked with delight and ran to Hanna and hugged her.

'Oh God, I'm sorry, Hanna,' Emma said, releasing Hanna as quickly as she had grabbed hold of her. 'I didn't mean to do that, but I couldn't help myself. I'm a huge fan. And no. That isn't how I usually greet famous artists. But when Russell said you were a friend, I sort of forgot myself in my excitement.'

'Don't worry about it, Emma. Any friend of Russell's is a friend of mine. It's lovely to meet you.' Hanna glanced around at the stunning art hanging on the walls. 'I'm impressed. This is the perfect space. I'd be happy to see my art here.'

'Would you? Would you really?' Emma beamed at Russell. 'I know this isn't the time to ask this, but do you mean that, Hanna? Would you consider allowing me to exhibit some of your paintings? Or even one would be fantastic.'

'Yes. Of course.'

Russell was a little anxious. He had known Emma was a fan, of course, but he hadn't considered that she might ask to exhibit Hanna's paintings, although obviously, he should have. Fortunately, Hanna didn't seem to mind. Or if she did, she was good at hiding her feelings.

'I hope Emma didn't put you on the spot,' he said, as they left for home later that afternoon. 'It didn't occur to me that she might do that.'

'It's not a problem. Emma is lovely and the gallery is wonderful. I'm happy to do it.

She's going to give me a call next week to discuss it further.'

'I'm glad you liked it. I must admit, it's larger than I'd expected and she did have some fantastic artwork. None as good as yours, of course.'

'Naturally,' Hanna laughed. 'That goes without saying.' And then she swivelled in her seat and beamed at him. 'It's been a brilliant day, Russell. Thank you for asking me to join you.'

'You're very welcome,' he said, as his heart thumped in his chest. 'I've really enjoyed it too. Erm. I don't suppose you're free tomorrow, are you?'

She looked surprised, but then again, he was surprised he'd said it.

'Tomorrow? Erm. Yes. I could be. What did you have in mind?'

He couldn't tell her what was on his mind right now. He wanted to pull the car over, take her in his arms, and kiss her. But obviously, he couldn't do that.

He coughed and furrowed his brows. 'Lunch in Folkestone? We could wander around the market and then have a drink or two at The Lighthouse Champagne Bar, followed by lunch in a little Italian restaurant I know. The place might be small but the food is the best you'll eat this side of Italy. I seem to remember from our conversation at Easter that you love Italian food.'

She raised her brows. 'You remembered that?'

'I love it too, so it wasn't difficult. Does that sound good?'

'It sounds perfect.'

'Great! So that's a date then.'

'That's a date,' she said, and there was something in her tone that made him think it might be.

It was just as well he hadn't mumbled that he hadn't meant to say it was a date. He didn't want to scare her off.

But she didn't seem scared. In fact, if he didn't know better, he might think she was as eager about this 'date' as he was.

Twelve

For one brief and wonderful moment Hanna had thought Russell was going to kiss her when he'd dropped her off yesterday evening. But, of course, he hadn't. Had she been imagining the looks he had given her throughout that glorious day? Or were those looks of empathy, not of something else entirely? Did he feel merely friendship and compassion for her, even though she was sure she had seen a hint of something more in his eyes?

She'd considered inviting him in, but an odd feeling in the pit of her stomach had stopped her. She didn't want to push her luck, and having him in her cottage on a sultry summer evening, or sitting in the garden with him, drinking chilled white wine, and watching another beautiful sunset like the one the night before, might have made her forget herself. She might have asked him to stay. And if she'd done that, there was a very good chance he'd have run in the opposite direction.

The only thing she really knew for sure about Russell's love life was that he was in love with Hope for some time. She'd heard that he'd had girlfriends in the past and, unlike Griff, some of Russell's had lasted for more than a few weeks. One or two had lasted for a couple of years. Also, unlike Griff, no one mentioned Russell having one night stands. Griff, on the other hand, seemed to attract women like moths to a flame, and most of those women got burnt. But, of course, that had been because Griff had been in love with Grace for most of his life, and no other woman had ever meant anything to him.

Russell had told Hanna yesterday that he was completely over Hope. He hadn't said he'd met someone new. Did that mean he was free to fall in love again? And would he? Or would he decide it was time he played the field? Would a hook up with Hanna, even for one night, be something he might consider?

But she didn't want one night of sex with him. Although if that was all she could get, would she say no? She wanted more though. Much, much more. And that, of course, was the problem. She wanted him to love her. To want her. To need her. To be unable to imagine his life without her by his side.

That's how Griff felt about Grace. Could Russell ever feel that about Hanna?

Or would he always just think of her as a friend?

Or worse still, someone to pity?

That thought deflated her a little, but she soon pulled herself together. She had today to look forward to.

Russell had sent her a text last night to wish her pleasant dreams. Which had worked, because she'd spent all night dreaming about him. He'd also said in his text that he'd pick her up around eleven a.m., which was later than she'd hoped.

But the sky was blue, the sun was shining, the birds were singing, what more could she ask for? For now, at least.

Russell looked gorgeous and the sight of him had taken her breath away for a second as she'd opened the front door. His golden blond hair seemed to shimmer in the sunlight even more this morning, and those beautiful blue eyes sparkled so brightly when he looked at her, that she had to look away. She quickly took in how his navy blue trousers hugged his hips, and how his pale blue T-shirt clung to his perfect torso. She was sure she could see the outline of a perfect six-pack beneath that cotton T-shirt and for a moment all she could think of was peeling it off him and running her hands over his bare flesh.

'Are you okay?' he asked, concern evident in his voice as he'd clearly mistaken her quiver of delight at the thought of him naked, as a shiver. 'You didn't catch a chill yesterday did you?'

'No. I feel great, thanks.'

She felt even better as the day progressed.

Folkestone was heaving with locals and tourists alike, and the market was full to bursting as everyone jostled against one another. She had never seen the place so crowded. Russell took her hand so that they wouldn't get separated in the throng, and at one point, he even put his arm around her in a protective fashion.

'This is crazy,' he said. 'Shall we get out of here?'

She hesitated for a moment. Would he let go of her if they did? An elbow in her back made her mind up.

'Good idea. At this rate, we'll be black and blue all over.'

Their eyes met briefly. Had he had the same thought as she had in that second?

She'd like to see every inch of him, black and blue, or tanned and white.

'This way,' he said, with a distinct catch in his voice.

The Harbour Arm was just as crowded

and they decided to give The Lighthouse Champagne Bar a miss and head directly to the Italian restaurant.

'There's a garden at the rear,' he said, 'so we can sit out there instead. The view might not be quite as scenic, although as I'll be sitting opposite you, it will be for me.'

She almost wished he wouldn't say things like that. Unless he meant them. And he didn't, of course. She knew that.

He had been honest about the food though. It was the best platter of antipasti she had ever tasted and the colourful, bite sized delicacies were displayed like a work of art. Fresh seasonal fruits and vegetables were sliced, diced, or left whole in the case of grapes. Fried courgette strips, sweet roasted and diced red peppers, marinated olives and artichoke hearts, plump little balls of mozzarella, slices of gorgonzola, creamy fontina, and a nutty and flavoursome Pecorino Romano, along with salami, prosciutto and capicola all vied for attention. Warm, toasted bruschetta with melting Gorgonzola, topped with Parma ham and honey, and sautéed prawns with garlic and chilli also tempted the taste buds. That first course alone was enough to fill Hanna up, but the main course she had chosen of baked salmon with a pistachio, honey, and herb crust served with artichokes braised in white wine, was to die for. She couldn't manage dessert and neither could Russell, who had eaten the same main course as she had, but he had added Italian roast potatoes.

'We'll have to come back another time and have dessert,' he said, when Hanna told him she was full. 'Or stay here all day and wait until we're hungry again.'

'I don't think I could eat another mouthful until tomorrow.' She leant back in her chair and puffed out her cheeks, and then, realising that that wasn't the most attractive pose to adopt, she sat upright.

'Same here. I'd suggest we come back tomorrow but it's the Summer Fayre this weekend so I need to be there.'

How had she forgotten about the Summer Fayre? Not only was it an annual event in Betancourt Bay, held in the grounds of Betancourt itself, there were posters and flyers plastered everywhere promoting it. Even here in Folkestone. Not only that, Russell had already told her he had come home especially for it. And Grace and Hope had told her weeks ago that Griff had employed Eversley Events to be in charge of the catering this year.

The annual Summer Fayre was for charity, and was paid for by the Betancourts. Colourful marquees and stalls were erected on the wide front lawns of Betancourt, either side of the long drive, and dotted around the sprawling grounds. One area of lawn was set aside for croquet; another for a friendly game of cricket; and yet another for various races or games, like an egg and spoon race, or a sack race, or a pass the balloon under your chin race, or even a tug of war.

And then there were the friendly competitions, like the best sponge cake, or the largest marrow, or the most amusingly misshapen vegetable. There was a Punch and Judy booth, a bouncy Castle, and a Fortune Teller's tent. An ice cream van, a Candy Floss machine, and a hot Dog stand were hired in, but other than those, all the food was provided by caterers hired by the Betancourts, although this year, Eversley Events were handling that on the Betancourt's behalf.

Most of the stalls were set up on the front lawns each year, along with all the games and other entertainments, but afternoon tea was taken in the beautiful gardens at the rear of the house which were always resplendent and brimming with colour.

A large, white Marquee was set up there, between the heavenly scented rose garden and the formal knot garden, and in addition to afternoon tea, champagne and canapes were on offer later in the day.

Tables and chairs for two, four, or six,

were set up on the raised terrace running the width of the rear of the house, and beyond the York stone steps which led down to the rest of the garden, more tables and chairs could be found either side of a broad path that zig-zagged to the left and right at various intervals, down the centre of the garden, as far as the eye could see. There was additional seating available around the large lake, with its tall fountain almost as grand as the one on Lake Geneva.

The lawns to the rear weren't as manicured as those to the front and were dotted here and there with more shrubs and trees, some of which provided shade for the tables and chairs.

On each side sat a copse of trees, and a mini treasure hunt was set up, with clues tied to the branches. The wildflower garden was a popular place for people to stroll through via the designated paths and the only area that was strictly out of bounds was the kitchen garden to the left of the house.

'There's going to be one small difference this year,' Russell said. 'Now that Dad's acquired several chickens, and also recently added some Indian Runner ducks, he's agreed that the kitchen garden won't be off limits. At least, part of it won't. The youngsters will no doubt enjoy cuddling a hen, and laughing as the ducks waddle around. I was watching them last night and they're so funny.'

'Yes,' Hanna said. 'I saw them a couple of weeks ago just after they arrived. They're adorable. And I don't think it'll only be the youngsters who'll want to cuddle the hens and watch the ducks. Will the gates at the top of the cliff be open this year? Didn't someone try to climb over them last year?'

Russell rolled his eyes. 'Yes. There's always one idiot who drinks far too much and then thinks he's invincible. But no. The gates will be locked as always. And this year Griff has organised a larger sign warning of the danger. The private steps down to the beach are safe, but if you don't stick to the path, those cliffs can be lethal. It's better to be safe than sorry, especially as dogs are welcomed to the Summer Fayre. The last thing we'd want is for a dog to go charging over the edge. Or for a person, obviously.'

'You're excited about it, aren't you?'

'The Summer Fayre? Yes. I am. Apart from earning quite a bit for charity, it's a fun weekend. Everyone in the village loves it, and people come from miles away to attend. It wouldn't be summer without the Betancourt Summer Fayre. Just like it wouldn't be Christmas without The Mistletoe Dance. You will be coming, won't you?'

'To the Summer Fayre?' Hanna shook

her head. 'I don't know.' She was loathe to bring the subject up but he would no doubt ask why she was unsure about it, and what else could she say? He beat her to it.

'If it's because of the gossip, I think you should ignore that and show your face.'

Their eyes met and she found it difficult to look away.

'That's easy for you to say. The gossip isn't about you.'

'It was at Christmas, and at the New Year, and on Valentine's Day, and even at Easter, so I know exactly what it's like. But I still showed my face, Hanna.'

She raised her brows at him. 'You also spent as much time in London, or travelling for work, as you could. You weren't here every day.'

'That's true. But that wasn't because of the gossip. That was because I needed to get over Hope, and seeing her every day made that harder to do. Being away from her, and also, if I'm honest, not having to see my brother and Grace so madly in love each day, helped. When your heart is broken, the last thing you want to be around is couples who are deeply in love.' He blanched and his brows knit together. 'Oh God. Sorry. I shouldn't have mentioned them.'

'Why not? Oh! Yes. Erm. Because ... because of the gossip about me.' She had to think quickly. 'But that's why I think I should stay away from the Summer Fayre. To ... to avoid seeing ... them.'

'So it is true then?' He sounded annoyed and upset. 'I didn't think it was. Or maybe I just hoped it wasn't. But you ... you're saying it is? You're in love? With Griff?'

'Erm. I'm in love.'

'Excuse me,' he said, getting up so fast it startled her. 'I ... I need to nip to the loo.'

Hanna wanted to burst into tears.

Thirteen

He only had himself to blame. Barbra Brimble had said that she had heard Hanna say it, with her own ears, and from Hanna's own lips, and yet he hadn't believed it. Now Hanna had said it to his face. Hanna was in love with Griff and there wasn't a damn thing Russell could do about it.

He splashed cold water on his face. He took several deep breaths. He even let out a silent scream, but nothing made him feel better. He paced to and fro across the black and gold tiled floor of the men's lavatories for several minutes, but still he didn't feel in control.

Yet again, the woman he loved, wasn't in love with him. Only this time it was even worse. This time the woman was in love with his brother.

But Hanna's love for Griff was as unrequited as his love had been for Hope. Griff would be kind, of course, although

Grace might not be, but somehow, Hanna had to get over this.

Russell had told her he would help. He'd told her he was her friend. But that was when he didn't believe it was true.

He stared at his reflection in the mirror over the row of three white porcelain sinks. 'Well now you know it is. And it serves you right.'

He took more deep breaths and he clenched his hands beneath the cold water.

He *was* Hanna's friend. So now he had to act like it.

He cleared his throat, practised a caring – but not pitying – smile, dried his hands beneath the warm air dryer, and marched back to their table.

His friend Luigi, the owner of the restaurant stood in his path. Luigi shrugged his shoulders and made a sad face. 'The Lady, she ask me to give you this,' Luigi told him in broken English as he handed Russell a folded piece of paper.

Russell shot a look at the now empty seat where he had left Hanna sitting, and hastily read the note.

'I'm so sorry, Russell. Please don't come after me. I need to be alone. Thank you, for being you.'

'She has left,' Luigi added. 'You love her, no? Ah, Love. It is not always kind. Come.

Drink with me. We will drown our sorrows, no?'

Russell stared at the glass door for a moment, torn between racing after Hanna, or staying where he was and getting drunk.

She had asked him not to go after her, so the second option was as good as any right now.

'Yes,' Russell said, following Luigi to a different table. The man was nothing if not tactful. 'But I'm not sure there's a wine vat big enough to drown my sorrows.'

Fourteen

Hanna was fortunate to get a cab as quickly as she did. The crowds were still as bad as they had been earlier, although, oddly enough, the traffic from Folkestone to Betancourt Bay was light.

During the short journey she formulated a plan. It was dramatic, probably foolish, and possibly the wrong thing to do, but she couldn't face Russell again for a while. The look on his face when she'd said she was in love, had been one of abject horror. Mingled with shock. Tinged with anger. And full of disappointment. So many emotions all rolled into one. And he'd got up and walked away. Albeit, she had assumed, temporarily.

She hadn't actually told Russell she loved Griff, of course, but she had admitted to being in love, and Russell had jumped to the same conclusion as everyone else had. What she should've said was, 'No. I'm not in love with Griff. But yes. I am in love.' Or maybe just the first bit. But then how would she have explained what Barbra had heard her say? And she had said those words. But she hadn't mentioned Griff. It was Russell she had been alluding to, not his older brother.

Obviously, she couldn't admit that to Russell. Or to anyone. So she shouldn't have admitted to being in love. She should've denied it all.

But she should've done that on Wednesday. It was too late for that now.

She would take a leaf out of Russell's book. She would leave Betancourt Bay for a while.

Oak Street was empty when the cab pulled up and she leapt out and dashed into Catkin Cottage. It didn't take her long to throw some clothes and toiletries into a couple of large holdalls.

The cab driver gasped in surprise when she threw them into the back of his cab, and chuckled as she climbed in after them. 'I was just nodding off! That was fast. When you said you'd be five minutes, I thought you were working on the same time frame as my darling wife. Which basically means twenty.'

'I've got a train to catch,' Hanna said, 'so if you can make this cab go faster, I'd appreciate it.'

'Right you are,' he said, and she fell back

against the padded seat as he sped away. 'Off to somewhere nice?'

'London. Sorry. I need to make a call.'

She dialled the number and crossed her fingers. She didn't have anywhere else she could go.

Fifteen

'Hello, Hanna. This is a surprise. You haven't changed a bit.'

'Hello, Aunt Susan. Neither have you. I apologise for this, but I had nowhere else to go.'

'All the hotels are full then, are they? No. Don't turn away. I told you when you called that you are more than welcome, and I meant it. Come in.'

'Thank you. I did consider an hotel, but I didn't want to be alone right now.'

Hanna stepped inside Susan's terraced Victorian, two-storey house in Wimbledon Village in South West London. A house she hadn't been inside since the day she had walked out of it more than twelve years ago.

'Drop your bags there. We'll sort those out later. I'll open a bottle of wine and you can tell me all about him.'

'Him? What makes you think there's a man involved?' Hanna dropped her holdalls beside an Edwardian coat stand but stayed where she was.

Susan glanced back over her shoulder and rolled her eyes. 'Oh, sweetheart. There's always a man involved. You've coped with anything and everything life threw at you, but when it involved a man, you always fell apart. And you wouldn't be here unless you were falling apart. Now follow me.'

'Well, you should know. You were the reason I fell apart the last time.'

Hanna didn't move. This was a mistake. A huge mistake.

Susan turned and walked back to her, and then she linked an arm through Hanna's, and coaxed her forward.

'Are we still doing that? I thought that hatchet was buried when you finally answered my calls two years ago. If this is going to be a problem you need to say so now, because, despite what everyone said at the time, we're still together you know.'

'But he's not here, right? You told me when we spoke that he wasn't here.'

'Don't panic. He's not. Would it still bother you to see him? You told me you got over him years ago.'

'I did. I am. But … I'm feeling vulnerable right now and … and even being here is bringing it all back. I should go. This was a mistake.'

'Stop being such a drama Queen, young lady.' Susan unlinked their arms and placed both her hands on Hanna's shoulders, forcing her to sit. 'Sit down and breathe, for heaven's sake. Whoever this man is, you've got it bad, haven't you? Now stay. I'm opening the wine and we're going to drink and talk and sort this all out.'

Hanna took several deep breaths. Susan might have broken Hanna's heart all those years ago, but something deep inside had told Hanna to come here.

She glanced around, only now realising they were in a large open plan kitchen, dining, and sitting room. The grey kitchen units were all sleek lines, like Susan herself, and the dining and sitting areas had modern, grey, and no doubt designer, furniture. The TV, wherever it was, was hidden from view, and there wasn't a single book in sight, which was odd. Hanna remembered the house being full of books. Now the pale grey walls were covered with possibly hundreds of paintings. Black framed, glass folding doors led out onto a dark grey slate patio and beyond that a beautifully manicured lawn with flower borders, and silver birch trees, all bathed in a purple glow from the outside lights. Two equally sleek Russian Blue cats strolled down a path as if they were on a fashion cat walk, and Hanna gave a quiet snort. Even the cats were grey. But grey had always been Susan's favourite colour.

'So what do you think of the place?' Susan asked from the kitchen area, and Hanna had to swivel in her dark grey chair to face her.

'It's grey,' Hanna said. 'But it's beautiful. You've made several changes. Like knocking three rooms into one. Where have all the books gone?'

'We have a library now. And a study. We've gone up into the loft space to make room for those.'

'Still writing self-help books?'

'Still painting? Some things will never change.' Susan handed Hanna a glass of chilled white wine. A large glass. She clinked her glass with Hanna's. 'Cheers. It's lovely to see you after so many years. Did you spot them?'

Hanna took several large gulps of her wine. She needed them. 'Spot what? The cats? Yes. They're also beautiful. But … he was allergic to cats, wasn't he?'

A slow grin spread across Susan's generous mouth as she sat in another dark grey chair opposite.

'Still is. But he's grown used to them. Sadly, the same can't be said for them. They hiss at him. Then again, so do I sometimes. I didn't mean the cats. I meant the paintings.'

'I could hardly miss them, could I? Since when did you become such an art lover? I seem to remember bare walls, save for a few large and impressive mirrors here and there.'

'Mirrors are for young people. Once you hit sixty, they're not always so kind. Art is far more beautiful to look at than my reflection, I've realised.' She took a sip of wine. 'Especially your art.'

'My art!' Hanna's gaze shot around the room. She'd thought a few of the paintings were familiar but there was no way Susan would've bought any of hers.

And yet.

Now she looked at them, more than half of them were hers.

'I'm proud of you, Hanna. You're an extremely talented artist.'

'Thank you,' Hanna replied, for want of anything else to say. She took more gulps of wine.

Susan ran a slim finger around the rim of her glass. 'I am sorry that things turned out the way they did. But I've always been a selfish person. You knew that. I haven't changed on that score. We can't choose whom we love. And as I've said, more than once, you and he wouldn't have stayed together. You simply weren't right for one another.'

'So you still think you did me a favour by

stealing my boyfriend. Even though it broke my heart, and, as you said, I fell apart. That was okay, because you loved him and he loved you.'

Hanna had never told anyone in Betancourt Bay about Jeremy. Or about Susan. She'd pushed them to the back of her mind and tried to pretend they didn't exist. She'd never said she was once in love with a man who had fallen in love with her aunt. An aunt who was twenty-five years her senior. And twenty years older than the man she had loved. Being dumped for another woman was bad enough. Being dumped for a woman twenty-five years older, who was a blood relative of yours, wasn't something Hanna wanted to shout about. Although, at the time, Hanna had done quite a lot of shouting. Jeremy had cried. Susan had simply hugged her and told her how sorry she was, and how much she loved Hanna. But that she loved Jeremy too.

'It wasn't okay. No. But I had to choose. And rightly or wrongly I chose him. You weren't the only one who's heart broke that day. But I would still choose him, if I had to do it all over again. As ridiculous as it sounds, we're soul mates, Hanna. We're like two parts of a machine. Neither of us work if we're apart for long, but together we can move mountains. When you find the right man, you'll understand that sometimes a love comes along that you'd die for. That you'd give up anything and everything for. And I think you feel you've found that man. You wouldn't be here if you hadn't. Let's not dwell on the past. That's water under the bridge and there's no going back. Let's look to the present and the future. So, what's the problem?'

Hanna emptied her wine glass in large gulps and held it out to Susan who raised one delicate brow and gracefully stood up and almost floated across the floor to get the bottle of wine. She returned with two bottles; the open one and another, and she refilled Hanna's glass, and then sat back down in her chair.

'The problem is, he doesn't love me.'

'I see. Yes. That could be a problem. But it's not insurmountable if he's the right man. Tell me all about it. Tell me what brought you here.'

Hanna told Susan the entire story, beginning with how Russell had been in love with Hope. She started her story at Christmas Eve and the Mistletoe Dance, and almost twenty minutes later, without Susan saying another word, she finished it at the train station to come here.

'Well. Assuming you've told me everything, I'd say you're in the wrong place.'

Hanna let out a long and sorrowful sigh. 'I thought that too. I knew I shouldn't have come. But ... I couldn't think of anyone else to talk to about this. My friends are all so involved and they'd tell Russell how I felt and that ... that would only make things worse.'

'I meant,' said Susan, refilling Hanna's glass from the newly opened bottle. 'That where you should be is standing in front of Russell telling him you love him.'

'What? Haven't you heard what I've said?'

'Every single word. And I repeat, you should be telling him you love him. But I suppose there's no rush. He's not going anywhere. You're here now and I'd love you to stay for a day or two. For longer, if you like. We need to mend some bridges. And I've missed you, Hanna. I really have. You don't love Jeremy, so, although you may never forgive us entirely, for what we did, surely you can find it in that huge heart of yours to tolerate us? He won't be back until next week, so why don't you stay and we can see how things go? Oh. I do have one question about Russell though. How many times has he called you since you left him at the restaurant?'

Hanna shrugged as tears pricked her eyes. 'I ... I don't know. I think I left my phone in the cab to Folkestone station. I didn't notice it was missing until I was on the train.'

'Oh, sweetheart. Why didn't you say so? We'll call the cab office and see if it's there. If not, the first thing we'll do tomorrow is get you a new phone and get your number transferred. Don't worry. It's not the end of the world.'

'Really?' Hanna sobbed. 'It feels like it is.'

Sixteen

'Yoo-hoo! Grace!'

Grace turned as she heard her name, and quickly wished she hadn't. The last person she wanted to see today was Barbra Brimble. She gave the woman a brief wave and marched off in the opposite direction.

Griff had just finished his speech to declare the Betancourt Summer Fayre officially open and he was now mingling with the crowds, as were Russell, Archie, and Tabby. Grace was meant to be mingling too, but she wasn't feeling particularly jolly this morning.

The same could be said for Russell. He had been like a bear with a sore head ever since he'd come home drunk last night. So drunk that Griff had had to help him into bed. Yet there he was, doing his bit as a Betancourt, pretending everything was fine.

Well it was far from fine, and Grace was fairly certain that whatever Barbra wanted to say, would only make things worse. She would avoid the woman for as long as she could.

At least Grace now knew the truth about the gossip concerning Hanna and Griff. In his drunken stupor last night, Russell had announced that all the gossip was true. That Hanna had told him so herself that very afternoon. She did love Griff.

'I've been a fool,' he'd said. 'A complete and utter idiot. I've been blind and stupid, and so have all of you. We all have. Hanna loves Griff. She said so. And then she left. Just like that. And now she won't answer her phone. Or her door. I stopped at her cottage on the way home and it was dark. All dark. Was she hiding? Who knows?' He collapsed onto the sofa. 'She loves Griff. How did I not see that? Why did I think that maybe, just maybe, she might ... she might. Who cares? Not me. Been there, done that, got the T-shirt and the badge.'

'What did she tell you?' Grace had asked.

'That she loves Griff,' he'd replied.

'Did she just come right out with it?'

'She said she loves Griff,' he'd repeated.

'We're not going to get much sense out of him tonight,' Griff had said. 'Come on, Russell. I'm taking you to your room.'

They hadn't got much sense out of him this morning at breakfast either.

'I've got the headache from Hell and I don't want to talk unless it's a matter of life or death. I definitely don't want to talk about Hanna Shaw. I've said all I've got to say on that subject. She loves Griff. She said so. Now you have your answer.'

No matter how much Grace had tried to coax him to elaborate, his lips were sealed. He'd even made a zipping gesture with his forefinger and thumb by swiping them along his lips, and then he'd got up and gone back to his room, saying, 'Wake me half an hour before we open the gates for the Summer Fayre, please.'

'Will do,' said Griff.

'Is that it?' Grace snapped.

'I think we should leave it be, darling,' Griff said. 'What we must decide now is how we intend to deal with this. I think we should give her time. She knows you're the only woman I've ever loved and ever will love, so she knows she needs to get over whatever it is she thinks she feels. I'm still not convinced she loves me. But she is coming to our wedding, and if you'd rather she didn't, then now is the time to tell her. In the nicest way we can.'

'She's not coming. Definitely not. I know we can't choose who we love, and I do like her. I really do. And I feel sorry for her. But this wedding should be a beautiful day, and it won't be if I'm worried about what she might do or what she might say.'

'Then we'll tell her. I'm sure she'll understand. She may decide she doesn't want to be there in any event. She's usually such a sensible person. I don't understand this at all. But don't worry, darling. We'll sort this out. I'll sort this out. I'll go and have a chat with her later today. For now, we must concentrate on making this year's Summer Fayre the best one yet.'

Grace wasn't certain that she liked the idea of Griff seeing Hanna alone. Not because she didn't trust him. She did. But if anyone saw him go inside Catkin Cottage, there'd be a whole new batch of gossip by tomorrow.

So here they all were, on the manicured lawns of Betancourt, pretending they were having fun. At least Grace was pretending. She was searching the crowds for Hanna, and would be all day, just in case Hanna turned up.

'Grace! There you are!' It was Barbra's voice. And the woman was right behind her. Grace closed her eyes, took a deep breath, and turned around to face the person who had started all the gossip.

'Hello, Barbra. I'm a little busy today so I don't have time for a chat.'

'I'm sure you are, dear, but I just wanted

you to know how pleased we all are that Hanna has done the right thing.'

'Done ... done the right thing? What does that mean?'

'That she's left the village! Didn't you know? Of course no one knows how long she'll be gone, but she had two large holdalls when she got back in the cab yesterday afternoon. That young girl, Honesty, who works for Naomi Hart and Lucas Dove was putting some rubbish in the bins at Betancourt Bay Café and she saw Hanna arrive in the cab and dash inside her cottage. Honesty then came back out with a second bag of rubbish and that's when she saw Hanna get back in the cab with the two holdalls. She told Naomi. Vera and Rita Boot were in the café, and so was Daisy Copeland, so it's definitely true. It was just gone three-thirty when the cab drove away. They synchronised their watches.'

'Barbra,' Griff said, smiling broadly. 'How lovely to see you. But I hope you'll excuse us. I need my darling fiancée to help me with something.' He took Grace's hand in his and virtually dragged her away. 'I thought you'd need rescuing.'

'I thought I would too, but you'll never believe what she told me.'

Griff rolled his eyes. 'What now?'

'No! It's good news. Well, I think it is.

Hanna's left the village. She left yesterday afternoon. With two large holdalls. Honesty saw her, and she told Naomi. Rita and Vera Boot along with Daisy Copeland, all heard her say it.'

'Left? What does that mean? Left for the weekend? For a holiday? For good? This whole thing gets stranger by the day. I love this village with all my heart, but sometimes I wish people would simply mind their own business.'

'I'm glad they didn't this time. I'm so relieved, Griff! This means we can go ahead with our wedding and not have to worry about anyone spoiling our special day.'

'Nothing could spoil our wedding day,' he said, easing her into his arms.

'I can think of a few things that could. But this is the best news I've had since ... since ... well, since you told me you loved me.'

He arched his brows. 'Not since I proposed to you?'

'No. Because that wasn't news. That was a question. But if we're talking about happiness, then yes, that was my happiest day. So far.'

He beamed at her. 'And our wedding day will be my dream come true.'

'And mine, Griff. I dream of little else these days.'

'Get a room, you two,' said Hope, as Griff

and Grace were locked in a passionate kiss, and she laughed as they broke apart, adding. 'Sorry! But there are children present you know. Tom and I saw you talking to Barbra just now and were on our way to rescue you but Griff beat us to it.' Hope smiled at Tom who was holding her hand in his.

'Oh you won't believe what she said. I've just been telling Griff.'

'I think,' said Griff, 'if it's all the same with you, my darling, I'll leave you to tell Hope and Tom. Someone should tell Russell this news and I think it may be best coming from me.'

'Oh yes, of course. You tell Russell. I'll see you in a second.'

Seventeen

'Left! What do you mean, she's left?' When Griff had taken him to one side and said he had something to tell him, all sorts of things had whirled around in Russell's mind, but Hanna leaving the village wasn't one of them. 'Why? For how long? Where's she gone?'

'Those are all excellent questions, but I'm afraid I don't have the answers.' Griff shook his head. 'All I know is what I've told you. But there'll be someone in Betancourt Bay who knows, I'm sure. She wouldn't simply leave without telling anyone, would she?'

'Don't ask me? She left the restaurant yesterday without telling me.'

'Yes. But she left you a note. What did it say again? Did it give any hint of her planned departure?'

'None. It said "I'm so sorry, Russell. Please don't come after me. I need to be alone. Thank you, for being you." And that was it. Perhaps that's what she meant by needing to be alone.'

'Possibly. But she could be alone in Catkin Cottage if she wanted. I don't think we need to worry. She's a sensible woman. Usually. This whole thing is odd though, don't you agree? And I know she told you she loves me, but I still don't believe it. Tell me what she said, exactly, if you can remember.'

'Oh, I can remember. I'll never forget it. We were talking about the Summer Fayre and I asked her if she was coming. She said she wasn't because of the gossip, and I told her she should. We then discussed how I'd felt when everyone was gossiping about me, and she said I'd spent most of my time away from here, and that she wanted to avoid seeing you and Grace together so she should stay away this weekend. But she didn't say *go* away, just *stay* away. And that's when ... when I realised the gossip was true. I asked her if it was and she said yes.'

Griff frowned. 'Did she? Did she actually say, 'yes it's true', or did you just think she said it?'

'What? She said it. I said, "So it is true then? I didn't think it was. Or maybe I just hoped it wasn't. But you're saying it is? You're in love? With Griff?" And she said, "Erm. I'm in love." I don't think she could've made it any clearer than that.'

'Hmm. Let me get this straight. You asked her if the gossip was true, and then you asked her that again in a slightly different way. Then you asked her if she was in love, and finally you added, with Griff, is that correct? They were all separate sentences? All separate questions?'

'Yes. No. I don't see why that matters.'

Griff let out a sigh. 'Oh, Russell. Of course it matters. That's the problem with gossip and hearsay, and even with two people having a conversation but not actually hearing what the other person is saying.'

'I have no idea what you're saying right now. What matters? And why?'

'It matters because Hanna only answered one of your questions. And it wasn't the one, or should I say two, about the gossip being true. And it wasn't the one about me. You asked her if she was in love, and she told you she was.'

'Precisely! So what point are you trying to make here?'

'The point, brother dear, is that Hanna admitted she is in love. But she didn't tell you with whom she is in love. And at no time did she say the gossip was true. I was right all along. I knew there'd be a simple explanation, and there is. The problem now, of course, is that she has left the village and we have no idea where she's gone or for how long she may be away.'

'That's not the only problem. I still don't know what you're talking about but what I do know is that Hanna is in love, and that's a massive problem for me. Please don't tell anyone else about this yet, because after all that gossip about me and Hope, I'm not ready for another lot. But I think … No, I know–'

'That you're in love with Hanna. And probably have been for some time. Yes, Russell, I know.'

'What! How?'

Griff grinned. 'It's a talent of mine. I knew Grace was in love with me but I had to wait for her to realise she was. That took longer than I'd hoped. But sometimes these things do. And, if you remember, I knew you were in love with Hope. Although I think that, like Grace's former infatuation with you, what you felt for Hope was years of friendship that you manifested into what you believed was love. I saw you with Hanna at Easter, and the way you were together was completely different to the way you were around Hope. I was fairly sure then that you and Hanna had feelings for one another.'

'For one another? That's where you're wrong. I won't argue with you about my former feelings for Hope. I think I did love her, but now I'm over it. But I'll argue with you about Hanna having feelings for me. A couple of times I hoped she might, but clearly I was wrong. And I only knew myself this week, how strongly I felt about her.'

Griff sighed. 'Unless I'm mistaken – which I'm not, Hanna feels the same about you. It was you she was referring to when she said whatever it was to Barbra Brimble. Not me. You're the one who could make her dreams come true. Not me. You're the one she loves, Russell. Not me. She said so in the restaurant. You just weren't listening. She even said so in her note.'

'No she didn't. She doesn't love me. I know she ... Does she?'

'Yes.'

'Then why would she leave?'

'Because she thinks that you think that she's in love with me. And so does everyone else. She also probably thinks that if you had feelings for her, you'd tell her so. The reason she didn't immediately deny the gossip is because she knew part of it was true, and she didn't want to lie. But she couldn't say, 'I don't love Griff, I love Russell', could she? You were friends. She probably wanted to stay friends. She didn't want to scare you away with everyone in the village knowing how she felt about you. And that's why she didn't tell Grace. She knew Grace would never be able to keep that a secret from me.

And she didn't tell Hope because Hope would've told Grace. She probably wasn't sure she could tell anyone without them telling someone else. That's the problem with such close-knit communities. Someone always wants to tell someone something they think someone else should know.'

'I've been a fool, haven't I?'

'Yes, Russell, you have. But then so have I. It's taken me a while to understand all this. I must be losing my touch.'

'At least you haven't lost the woman you love.'

'Neither have you. Hanna will be back. I'm willing to bet on that.'

Eighteen

Hanna might have left her phone in the cab, but if she had, it had since vanished. The cab driver and the office staff checked the vehicle twice. Susan suggested Hanna should call the railway lost property office, just in case she had dropped the phone at the station, or on the train, but again, there was no sign of it, and nothing had been handed in. They notified her provider of the loss, and were told Hanna would be sent a new sim card, but getting it sent to Susan's home was a bit of a battle. Hanna had decided she would take up Susan's offer, and stay in Wimbledon Village for a few days.

The next day, she and Susan went to the shops and bought a new phone. It meant Hanna would have a different number for now, but at least she could download her contacts from Google, and once the new sim arrived, her provider would transfer her old number to the new phone.

In the meantime, Hanna sent a few emails on Saturday afternoon. She sent one to Grace, and one to Hope. She also sent one to Jemma who, along with Jemma's boyfriend, Greg, would be back in Oak Street in Betancourt Bay this weekend, and would no doubt be told all the gossip. Greg lived next door to the Boot twins, and Jemma was still renting Oak View Cottage, on the other side of Greg's cottage. Jemma would be moving in with Greg this coming week though, and, if the sale of Oak View Cottage went ahead, which it would, of that Hanna was certain, Tom would soon be moving in there, and Hope would be joining him.

Hanna's email to Grace read:

'Hi Grace. I hope the Summer Fayre is going well. I'm sorry I'm going to miss it this year. I'm also sorry I haven't spoken to you about the gossip concerning me and Griff. Not that there is a 'me and Griff', obviously. You know that. He adores you and only you. But I should've had the courage to come and talk to you. Actually, I should've had the courage to tell everyone right away that the gossip was wrong. Except it wasn't completely wrong. But we won't go into that right now. I just want you to know that although Griff is fantastic and I like him a lot as a friend, I am NOT in love with him. I never have been, and I never will be. But I am in love with someone else. Sadly that person is not in love with me. Anyway, I'm sorry to be such a bad friend. I should've spoken to you about this. I've left Betancourt Bay for a few days and am staying with a relative. I've lost my phone so I can't receive calls or messages and I need some time to think and clear my head, so I'm not giving out my new number. I will get my old one back soon, but, for now I'm contactable by email. Only in an emergency though, please. And yes, I know, I'm being a drama Queen, so I hope you'll forgive me for that. As I said, I need some time and space. I'm truly sorry, Grace. Please apologise to Griff for me too. And to Russell for running away. I'm a drama Queen and a coward, what can I say? Who knew? I think we could all use some space so I'm staying here for this week. I know it's your hen night next weekend and I'd still like to come to that. If you'll have me. I totally understand if you'd rather I didn't though so just email me next week and let me know what you decide. This is turning into a novel, and Jemma is the novelist among us, so I'll end this here. I hope I'm still invited to your wedding, but again, I understand if I'm not. Have fun at the Fayre. And give my love to everyone. I'm sending a similar email to Hope. And I'm also letting Jemma know what she'll be coming back to. Take care. Love, Hanna. Xx'

She sent a similar but not such a lengthy email to Hope, and a different one to Jemma, explaining that there was gossip in the village and what had happened since.

When she'd finished, she went and sat in the garden with Susan and the two Russian Blues, who were named, Catherine the Great, and Ivan the Terrible.

'They're Russian and they're Royal,' Susan said when Hanna arched her brows at the names. 'The cats are Russian Blues so it was that whole Royal blue blood thing that got me thinking the names were apt. Jeremy wanted to call them Fred and Ginger, and don't get me started on that.'

For years, Hanna hadn't spoken to Susan after the Jeremy fiasco and she had only let Susan know where she was because they were family and Hanna felt she had to. Susan had sent Hanna, Christmas and birthday cards every year, but Hanna had returned them unopened.

Two years ago though, Hanna had received a letter and it wasn't at Christmas, or anywhere near her birthday and she had instinctively known something was wrong.

The letter had been short, and had said, 'Hello Hanna. I hope you're keeping well, and I sincerely hope you're happy. Don't feel you need to respond to this letter, because you don't, but I have cancer. It's not going to kill me, believe me. And it doesn't change a thing between us. It was Jeremy who said you should know, just in case, so I'm telling you. I'm in the local hospital and they'll have operated by the time you receive this so don't come running up here and crying or anything like that. You know how much I hate that stuff. Anyway, I know it'll be fine and I'll probably outlive everyone I know. I love you, Hanna. If you feel like it, give me a call sometime this year, or next, or whenever. Or drop me a line. Don't send flowers. They should stay in the ground. Or chocolates. They make people fat. In fact, don't send anything. Bye then, Love Susan. Xx

Hanna had rushed to the hospital that day, but hadn't gone in to see Susan, once she'd ascertained where her aunt was. She had asked the nurse if all had gone well though, and had been told it had.

'Shall I give her a message?' the nurse had asked.

'No, thanks,' Hanna had replied, and then she had turned around and gone home to Betancourt Bay. She could've called and got the same news, but for some reason she had to be there, near to Susan but not too close.

She did reply to the letter a few days later saying that she hoped the operation had gone well, and that whilst she had no intention of calling Susan, if Susan wanted to call her, she wouldn't hang up.

A few months later, Susan had called her, and that's how they had started talking again. Not often and never for long, but they had exchanged civilities.

Hanna had never told Susan about her visit to the hospital that day, but now she did. And now they both cried and hugged and cried a little more. But they had drunk two bottles of wine again that evening, and they were both feeling somewhat emotional.

Hanna was just as emotional when she received emails from Grace, and from Hope, and from Jemma.

Jemma's email was one of surprise.

'Honestly, Hanna, my heart goes out to you. Some people can be so unkind. I have trolls on the internet so I know how awful it can make one feel, but surely no one in the village really believes it? We haven't yet returned to Betancourt Bay so Greg and I haven't heard the gossip, but the moment we do, we'll dismiss it as nonsense,' Jemma had written. 'Do let me know if you need anything, and I mean that. See you very soon, I hope. Love Jemma and Greg. Xx

Hope's had been ... well, Hope at her best.

'We're all friends, Hanna. We would've helped in any way we could. We weren't sure what to do though because you hadn't said it wasn't true and we were both confused. You needn't have run off! If you want to chat, we're here for you. We're both glad it's all sorted out now. See you at the hen night. It's going to be a lark. Grace doesn't know this yet, so don't say a word, but I've invited Vera and Rita Boot, as well as Granny Joy, and Daisy Copeland. And Tabby, obviously. And Mum, of course. But I've also invited Barbra Brimble because Mum said I had to if all the other oldies are coming. So you may want to bring a bat to hit her over the head with. Your choice entirely. Actually, the female population of Betancourt Bay will be there, so just ignore Barbra. I've taken a leaf out of the Boot sisters party book, and got the same male dancers slash strippers slash hot men wearing very little, as they had at their eightieth birthday bash. They got rave reviews. Make sure you've got lots of cash to stuff down their gold, sparkly pants. Oh, and we're having Salsa lessons from them too, so that should be ... enlightening. Griff said we can use the Great Hall at Betancourt, and he and Russell and Archie will sod off to London for the night, so Mum and I have organised a cocktail making and tasting session before the 'dancers' arrive, and a disco for afterwards because we girls love to dance. I've paid extra for the guys to stay on and ...

well, whatever. No sex, please, because we're British. HaHaHa! But anything else goes. There'll be food, of course, but you should line your stomach 'cos drink will be flowing all night. See you there. Love, Hope. Xx. P.S. I've bought a job lot of Alka-Seltzer and also Aspirin. Both will be in the party bags provided, along with a few other treats. Xx.'

Grace's had been short and sort of sweet.

'I'm the one who's been a bad friend. Even if you did love Griff, and most women do so I'm a little surprised you don't (only teasing) I should've worried less about me and thought more about you. I wish you'd tell me who this man – or person (I'm not judging) – is, but I'm sure you will when you're ready. Of course you must come to the hen night. And if you don't come to our wedding, there'll be trouble! I'll admit I did have concerns but that's because I'm a crazy woman right now. Hope says I make Bridezillas look like soft and fluffy kittens compared to me. I think she's planning something she shouldn't for the hen night, so let me know if you hear anything. Love you, Hanna. And Griff says he loves you too. But don't read anything into that because he's mine. All mine. All mine! Hahaha. Love, Grace. Xxx

The email that really surprised Hanna was one she received from Russell.

'I'm glad you're okay, Hanna. I was worried. Please never run off like that again. Talk to me, Hanna. I'm a friend. A good friend, I hope. Come home soon. I'd like to take you out for those desserts. And for a chat. Or whatever. Look after yourself. We miss you. Best wishes, Russell.

'That's romantic,' Susan said, looking over Hanna's shoulder.

'I told you he just sees me as a friend.'

'I disagree. I think there's a hidden message in there somewhere. Desserts are romantic. And a chat is better than 'we need to talk', so I think you may be surprised. The 'whatever' could mean anything, but I think it means a long romantic walk, or at least a kiss. Maybe more. I still maintain you should tell him how you feel. Maybe over those desserts.'

Nineteen

Hanna returned to Betancourt Bay the following Saturday afternoon, having spent just over a week with Susan. A week she had enjoyed far more than she had expected. She had even planned another visit, and this time, Jeremy would also be there.

It was time she put the past behind her. She had let this affect her life far more than she should have. She even admitted to herself that she had blown it out of all proportion. Yes, her boyfriend had fallen in love with her aunt and her aunt had fallen in love with him, but they didn't do it on purpose. They didn't set out to hurt her.

And it happened more than twelve years ago. Life was far too short to bear grudges. She should've done more, two years ago when the cancer scare had made her realise how much she still loved Susan. And when Susan had called, Hanna could've been warm and friendly, not cold and bitter. Things would be different from now on.

She was later getting home than she had planned due to cancellations on the trains, but would still be back in plenty of time to get ready for Grace's hen night.

Wait. Was that Russell going into St Gabriel's church as her cab had sped past?

What was he doing there at four-thirty on a Saturday afternoon? What was he doing there at all? Russell wasn't one to attend church other than for Midnight Mass on Christmas Eve and for a few special occasions like weddings, and such. Was he ... was he getting married?

Of course he wasn't. She was being stupid. But why was he there? On an errand for Griff, perhaps? This might be her chance. What better place to be alone with him than St Gabriel's church? But wasn't he supposed to be in London with Griff and Archie? Today was Grace's hen night.

Now she had to know what he was doing, and the moment the cab stopped at Catkin Cottage, she asked the driver to wait while she tossed her holdalls into the hall, and then she jumped back inside, and yelled, 'Take me to the church!'

'On time!' He sang back to her and grinned at her via the rear view mirror.

'Hilarious,' she said but she grinned and gave him a huge tip when he dropped her right outside the door.

She ran inside, her heels click-clacking on the stone floor and called out his name.

'Russell! Russell? Are you here? Oh!' She stopped in her tracks with a final and rather loud click-clack of her heels and stared at everyone, as they all stared back. Griff and Grace were standing face to face in front of Reverend Copeland, with Russell by Griff's side and Hope beside Grace, while Archie and Tabby and the rest of the Eversleys, along with Hope's boyfriend, Tom, sat in the pews.

'Are you ... are you getting married now?'

'No,' said Griff, grinning.

Hope burst out laughing. 'I told you this would happen, didn't I?' she teased Grace. 'We haven't got to the part about anyone having objections to the wedding yet, but stick around Hanna, we'll get there.'

'That's not funny,' said Russell, looking a little concerned.

'Is this ... is this some sort of weird hen night thing then?' Hanna couldn't get her head around it.

'No,' said Grace. 'It's our wedding rehearsal. We had to delay it from earlier in the week because the poor reverend was unwell, and today was the only time we could all be here.'

'Oh. Thank God.'

'If you didn't know this was the rehearsal,' Griff said, 'what made you come here, Hanna? And weren't you calling Russell's name?'

All eyes turned from her to Griff and back to her.

'I ... Erm ... I saw Russell come in and I wondered why he was here because Hope said you'd all be in London.'

'I see,' said Griff. 'Is that all?'

'Sorry? What? I ... Erm. Yes.'

'You didn't come racing in here to say something in particular to my brother then?'

'Griff!' Russell glared at him.

'No! Absolutely not. What could I possibly have to say to ... Oh sod it! Opps. Sorry vicar.' Susan had told her that, the moment Hanna saw Russell again she should march right up to him and tell him how she felt. And that was what she had planned to do when she'd seen him from the cab. Okay, so lots of others were here, but everyone in the village would soon hear about it anyway, so what the heck? She took a deep breath while everyone stared or mumbled or fidgeted, and Russell just looked as if he was glued to the spot.

'In case any of you are in any doubt, I don't love Griff, I love his brother. Yes. That's right. I love you, Russell, and even if you don't love me, I have to tell you how I feel because I'll explode if I don't. Or it'll eat away at me forever. I love you. There. I've said it.'

'Where's Barbra Brimble when you need her?' quipped Hope as everyone else, including Russell stayed silent.

Griff gave Russell a sharp nudge. 'Your turn,' he said.

'Oh. Yes. Erm.' A crease formed between Russell's brows but a smile was rapidly spreading across his mouth. 'You do? Are you sure?'

Hanna nodded frantically. 'Yes. I'm certain. I absolutely do.'

'That's fantastic news, because I love you.'

'You ... you do?'

'I do. Completely and utterly. With all my heart, in fact.'

Griff cleared his throat. 'They're stealing our lines, my darling.' He winked at Grace who was looking from Russell to Hanna as if she had no clue as to what was going on. 'But here's one for you, Russell. Don't just stand there like an idiot. You may now kiss your girlfriend.'

'Girlfriend? What? Ooooh. My girlfriend. My girlfriend! Yes.' He covered the distance between Hanna and himself in a matter of seconds. He took her hands in his, looked into her eyes, and beamed at her. There was a catch in his voice as he asked,

'May I?'

'Oh, yes please!' Hanna said, oblivious to the cheering and clapping and general hubbub now going on around them as they shared a passionate kiss, in the usually quiet little church of St Gabriel's.

Twenty

Grace's hen night didn't work out quite as Hope had planned, but everyone enjoyed it nevertheless. Due to the vicar being ill and the wedding rehearsal being postponed until that very afternoon, Griff and Russell and Archie had decided not to go to London after all. Instead, they were going to spend the evening with Tom in a rather posh hotel in Folkestone and have dinner and drinks, and wait until the hen night was over, whatever time that might be. And thanks to the rehearsal being further delayed due to Hanna's announcement, the new plan made even more sense to everyone.

'I'd rather sleep in my own bed, if that's okay with you, darling?' Griff asked Grace at the wedding rehearsal.

'Of course it is. I'd rather not spend the night without you anyway.'

'I have a feeling Russell won't let Hanna out of his sight for long tonight either,' added

Griff.

'I had no idea she loved Russell, or that he loved her. But I'm so happy for them. They look good together don't they?'

'They do.'

'How would you feel, Grace,' asked Hope, 'if we had the hen night as planned, but then invited our men to join us later, at say, midnight?'

'I think that would make it the perfect night,' Grace said.

Which meant that the male dancers Hope had hired for the hen night had more competition with the ladies at the end of the evening, than they might have ordinarily been used to.

But Vera and Rita Boot, and Daisy Copeland, and Granny Joy, and even Barbra Brimble, had a thoroughly enjoyable time.

Jemma made a few notes on her phone while the hen night was in full swing and before her boyfriend Greg joined her at midnight, with the other men.

'I think it's time some of the older women in my books had a bit more, shall we say, fun?' she told Hanna, laughing. 'At the moment it's mainly the younger ones who have wild and passionate sex, but judging by these women here tonight, it's never too late to admire and enjoy the male form.'

The village gossip the following day had,

of course, been about how Hanna and Russell had declared their love for one another in St Gabriel's church, and had even said the words, 'I do', which must mean that it wouldn't be long before they did.

But they weren't the only ones, tongues were wagging about. News had quickly spread about how, at Grace's hen night, Barbra Brimble had tried to remove a pair of gold, sparkly pants from one of the male dancers with her teeth. Sadly, she hadn't applied enough denture adhesive to keep her gnashers in place, and the man had danced around the Great Hall of Betancourt with a pair of dentures attached to his gold, sparkly pants, while the owner of said dentures crawled after him on her hands and knees.

Her long-suffering husband, Bernard, who had listened to his wife's sharp and wagging tongue all their married life, was not best pleased by this gossip.

And neither, it must be said, was Barbra.

But she did retrieve her teeth. Eventually.

Twenty-one

The weather could not have been better for Grace and Griff's wedding day. It was pleasantly warm but not too hot or muggy. The sky was blue and the sun shone all day. The breeze was cooling for the men in Morning Suits, but was gentle enough not to blow a strand of Grace's perfectly coiffed hair out of place.

Her beautiful up-do was styled by Molly Law, and her chief bridesmaid and sister, Hope's, was styled by Molly's mum, Nikki, who later styled Pat and Granny Joy's hair too.

Molly would soon be leaving the salon in Folkestone to join a cruise ship where she would be working as a hairdresser in the ship's beauty salon, and although Nikki was sad that her only daughter was leaving, not just the business, but also the family home, she was pleased that Molly was living her life to the full. Especially as Molly would have the money to do as she wanted, once the sale of Oak View Cottage to Hope's boyfriend, Tom, completed.

The wedding party also had manicures and pedicures, and a make up artist made Grace and Hope even more beautiful than their natural complexions usually did.

Grace's wedding dress was a snow-white, silk, satin, and handmade lace, fit and flare, strapless gown with a sweetheart neckline, and a handmade beaded lace, three-quarter-length-sleeved bolero, designed exclusively for her and costing a fortune.

The Eversleys were wealthy but not made of money, but Griff had insisted on covering the full cost of the wedding, including the dress, stating that the wedding was a gift to his future wife to thank her for marrying him.

Grace wore an intricately woven crown of wild flowers in her hair, picked that very morning by Griff's own hands from the wildflower garden at Betancourt and transported to the hair salon by Tabby.

Her bouquet was also from Betancourt but the blooms came from both the wildflower garden and the rose garden, and were selected by Grace and Tabby, together with a florist from Folkestone who was in charge of the flowers for St Gabriel's church, and for inside the house, and also for the magnificent Marquee in the garden.

The selection of flowers from the gardens of Griff's home wasn't about cost, it was a matter of sentiment. His beloved mother, Francesca had planted both the rose garden and the wild flower garden long before she died, and he had asked Grace if she would add some blooms from them to her bouquet.

Instead, Grace had declared that she wanted all the flowers she would wear and carry that day to come from Betancourt, and Griff had told her he had thought he couldn't love her more than he already did, and yet, she had proved him wrong. He adored her more than he thought possible, and he added that, if his mother were alive, she would adore Grace too.

The men's boutonnières were also from the Betancourt gardens and Griff and Russell, and even Archie, said they felt as if Francesca was with them for the wedding.

Only those invited would be at the church for the wedding at two p.m. that afternoon, and for the five-course meal in the dining room at Betancourt after, but the entire village, and colleagues from both families' businesses, and other friends, were invited to the celebrations in the Great Hall, the Marquee, and the garden, that evening.

Russell was Griff's best man and it amused him to see Griff so nervous.

'The only other time I've seen you like this was when you proposed to Grace.'

'I just want this day to be perfect,' Griff said. 'I would be happy to marry Grace in a shoe box, but this is her day, and I want the very best of everything for her.'

'It will be perfect,' Russell reassured him. 'And you'd need to find someone with massive feet, for you to marry Grace in a shoe box.'

Griff threw Russell a wide smile. 'You might be doing this before too long, if I'm any judge.'

Russell raised his brows in mock surprise. 'Getting married?'

'Yes. I've never seen you so happy.'

'I've never been so happy. I thought what I felt for Hope was love, but it's nothing compared to how I feel about Hanna. My feelings for Hope are like a handful of sand in a desert. My feelings for Hanna are the entire desert. Or, like a drop in the ocean, compared to the entire ocean.'

Griff gave Russell a congratulatory tap on the arm. 'I know what you mean. You love Hanna more than you thought you could ever love anyone.'

'Yes. I do. And speaking of, I do, we had better make our way to the church.'

St Gabriel's was resplendent in the sunshine; they could see the church from the house. Cars bedecked with flowers awaited them in the drive but Griff wanted to walk the few metres to the church, and Russell was happy to join him.

They smiled at one another as they strolled past The White House, where Grace was inside, getting ready. She had an even shorter distance to walk but a car would be outside her door at one fifty-five on the dot, and would take her and Simon Eversley to St Gabriel's, a mere few seconds away.

The flowers inside the church were stunning and their heavenly scents filled the air. Sunlight blazed through the stained glass windows, casting light and dark shadows and a kaleidoscope of colours over the floor and pews and the assembled guests as everyone greeted the bridegroom and the best man.

Russell took the opportunity to leave Griff's side for a moment and go to give Hanna a brief but loving kiss. They had hardly been apart since the day of the wedding rehearsal, and had spent their first night together after Grace's hen night. A night that had blown Russell's mind. Making love had never been as good as it had been that night, and since then, it had been even better. They'd spent all of Sunday in bed, and Russell had covered every inch of Hanna's beautiful body with kisses, as she had his.

And now, today in this church, he remembered what Griff had just said about it not being long before he too would be a bridegroom. He cast a secret wish skywards, that Griff might be right. Because the thought of marrying Hanna and spending his life with her was all he seemed to be able to think about for the entire week since that day of the wedding rehearsal.

'You look beautiful,' he said, looking deeply into her eyes.

'You too,' she said. 'This is going to be a beautiful wedding.'

'It is. And speaking of weddings, I know this isn't the time or the place, and we've only been dating for one week, but if you're not doing anything much for the rest of your life, would you consider spending it with me, do you think?'

He heard her gasp and saw the love in her eyes as they sparkled at him.

'Are you ... are you asking me what I think you're asking?'

'I am. But I'll ask you properly later.'

'Then yes. I will consider it. In fact, I don't have to consider it. I can tell you right now. I would love to spend the rest of my life with you.'

'That's excellent news. We'll discuss this in more detail later. I love you, Hanna.'

'And I love you, Russell. But don't you have to be over there? Not standing here holding my hand.'

'What? Oh yes.' He gave her another quick kiss and dashed off to stand beside Griff, just seconds before the musicians began playing the music Grace had chosen for her walk down the aisle. It was Pachelbel's Canon, or Canon in D as it was often called.

Such a beautiful piece of music for such a glorious day, and the look on Griff's face as Grace walked towards him, with her father by her side, said more than words ever could, matched only by the look on Grace's face, her eyes fixed firmly on Griff, the man who was about to become her husband. The man whom everyone could see Grace adored.

A tear sprung up at the corner of Hanna's eye. Griff looked gorgeous, and Grace was definitely a beautiful bride, but Hanna's gaze was drawn to Russell. She only had eyes for him.

Russell met her eyes and smiled his dazzling smile. A smile just for her. A smile that told her that he was thinking the same thing she was. That one day soon, in the not so distant future, Hanna Shaw would be walking down this very aisle in this very church to become Russell Betancourt's wife.

She didn't have a father to walk down the

aisle beside her, but she did have an aunt. An aunt who would happily perform such a duty.

And Hanna didn't care how much the village might gossip about how fast their marriage was, because as far as Hanna was concerned her own wedding day couldn't come fast enough.

And from what Russell had just said to her, it seemed he agreed wholeheartedly.

Coming soon

Christmas on Midwinter Lane

Share the gifts of friendship and love this Christmas

Noelle adores Christmas, unlike her frosty neighbours. Last December, she moved into the middle cottage in a row of three, and hers was the only one adorned with sparkling lights and glittery decorations. She's determined things will change this Christmas.

Adele has spent Christmas alone for longer than she cares to remember. Overweight, underpaid, and struggling to keep her home, the festive season is anything but festive for Adele. Why should this year be different?

Marcus now hates Christmas. Divorce papers landed on his mat this time last year, his ex-wife having left him the Christmas before. This Christmas she is marrying his former best friend. What reason is there to feel joyful?

Noelle believes Adele and Marcus have more in common than their hatred of the festive season. Playing match-maker won't be easy, but Noelle is hoping, at the very least, they'll share the gift of friendship.

And when a stranger rings her doorbell, Noelle may get a surprise gift of her own.

Stay in touch with

Emily Harvale

If you want to be the first to hear Emily's news, find out about book releases, see covers and maybe chat with other fans, there are a few options for you:

visit: www.emilyharvale.com

Or join her Facebook group for all of the above and to chat with others about her books:

www.emilyharvale.com/FacebookGroup

Alternatively, just come and say 'Hello' on social media:

 @EmilyHarvaleWriter

 @EmilyHarvale

 @EmilyHarvale

A Note from Emily

Thank you for reading this book. I really hope it brought a smile to your face. If so, I'd love it if you'd leave a short review on Amazon, or even just a rating.

And, maybe, tell your friends, or mention it on social media.

A little piece of my heart goes into all my books. I can't wait to bring you more stories that I hope will capture your heart, mind and imagination, allowing you to escape into a world of romance in some enticingly beautiful settings.

To see my books, or to sign up for my newsletter, please visit my website. The link is on the previous page.

I love chatting to readers, so pop over to Facebook or Instagram and say, 'Hello'. Or better yet, there's my lovely Facebook group for the latest book news, chats and general book-related fun. Again, you'll find details on the previous page.

Also by Emily Harvale

The Golf Widows' Club
Sailing Solo
Carole Singer's Christmas
Christmas Wishes
A Slippery Slope
The Perfect Christmas Plan
Be Mine
It Takes Two
Bells and Bows on Mistletoe Row

Lizzie Marshall series:
Highland Fling – book 1
Lizzie Marshall's Wedding – book 2

Goldebury Bay series:
Ninety Days of Summer – book 1
Ninety Steps to Summerhill – book 2
Ninety Days to Christmas – book 3

Hideaway Down series:
A Christmas Hideaway – book 1
Catch A Falling Star – book 2
Walking on Sunshine – book 3
Dancing in the Rain – book 4

Hall's Cross series
Deck the Halls – book 1
The Starlight Ball – book 2

Michaelmas Bay series
Christmas Secrets in Snowflake Cove – book 1
Blame it on the Moonlight – book 2

Lily Pond Lane series

The Cottage on Lily Pond Lane – four-part serial
Part One – New beginnings
Part Two – Summer secrets
Part Three – Autumn leaves
Part Four – Trick or treat
Christmas on Lily Pond Lane
Return to Lily Pond Lane
A Wedding on Lily Pond Lane
Secret Wishes and Summer Kisses on Lily Pond Lane

Wyntersleap series

Christmas at Wynter House – Book 1
New Beginnings at Wynter House – Book 2
A Wedding at Wynter House – Book 3
Love is in the Air – spin off

Merriment Bay series

Coming Home to Merriment Bay – Book 1
(four-part serial)
Part One – A Reunion
Part Two – Sparks Fly
Part Three – Christmas
Part Four – Starry Skies
Chasing Moonbeams in Merriment Bay – Book 2
Wedding Bells in Merriment Bay – Book 3

Seahorse Harbour series

Summer at my Sister's – book 1
Christmas at Aunt Elsie's – book 2
Just for Christmas – book 3
Tasty Treats at Seahorse Bites Café – book 4
Dreams and Schemes at The Seahorse Inn – book 5
Weddings and Reunions in Seahorse Harbour – book 6

Clementine Cove series

Christmas at Clementine Cove – book 1
Broken Hearts and Fresh Starts at Cove Café – book 2

Friendships Blossom in Clementine Cove – book 3

Norman Landing series

Saving Christmas – book 1
A not so secret Winter Wedding – book 2
Sunsets and Surprises at Seascape Café – book 3
A Date at the end of The Pier – book 4

Locke Isle series

A Summer Escape – book 1
Christmas on Locke Isle – book 2

Betancourt Bay series

That Mistletoe Moment – book 1
That Winter Night – book 2
That Special Something – book 3
That Summer Hideaway – book 4
That Secret Wish – book 5

To see a complete list of my books, or to sign up for my newsletter, go to www.emilyharvale.com/books

There's also an exclusive Facebook group for fans of my books. www.emilyharvale.com/FacebookGroup

Or scan the QR code below to see all my books on Amazon.

Printed in Great Britain
by Amazon